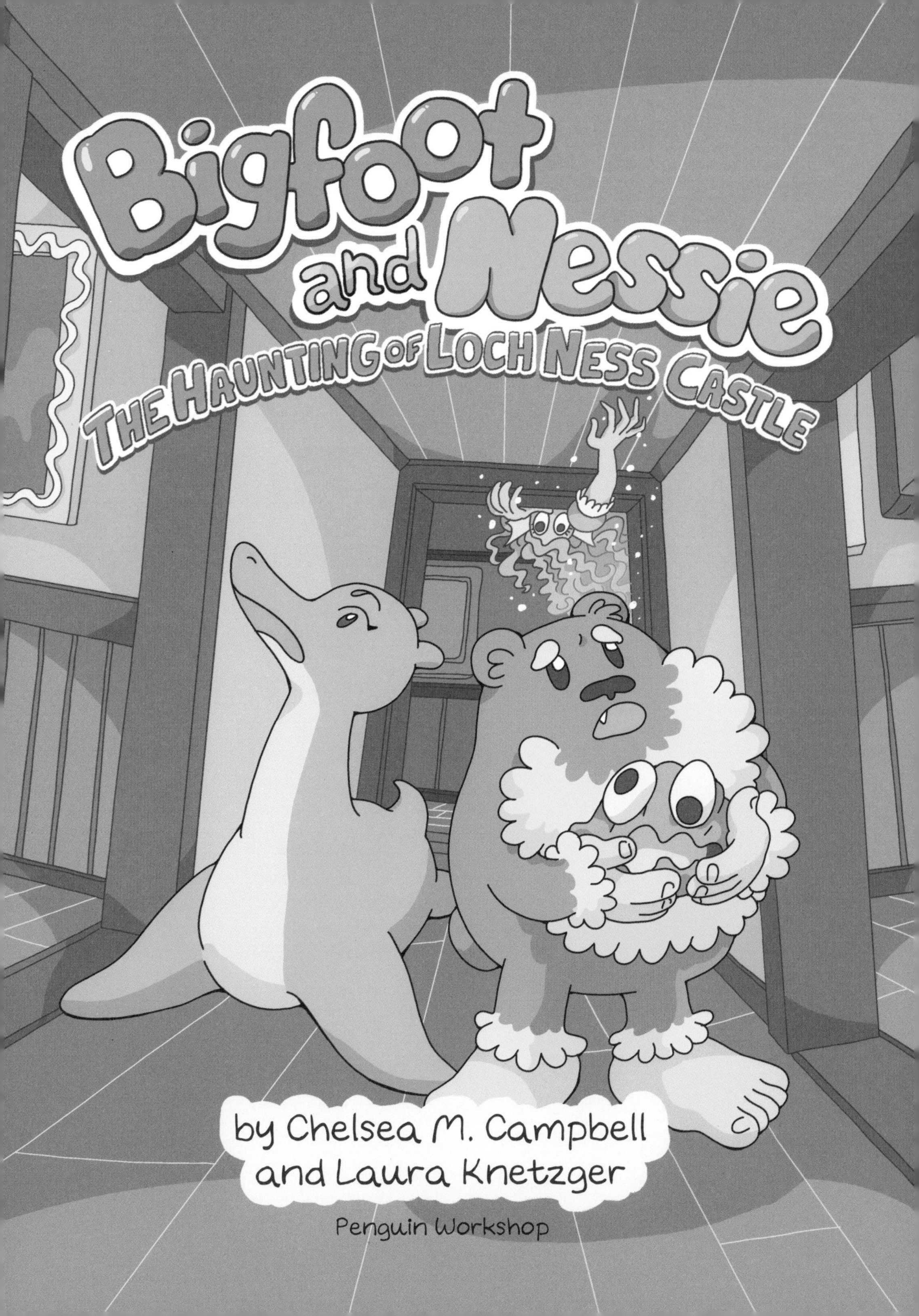

Bigfoot and Nessie

The Haunting of Loch Ness Castle

by Chelsea M. Campbell
and Laura Knetzger

Penguin Workshop

For Kitten, who is both extremely brave and extremely terrified of everything—CMC

For C—LK

PENGUIN WORKSHOP
An imprint of Penguin Random House LLC, New York

First published in the United States of America by Penguin Workshop,
an imprint of Penguin Random House LLC, New York, 2023

Visit us online at penguinrandomhouse.com.

Library of Congress Cataloging-in-Publication Data is available.

Manufactured in China

ISBN 9780593385753   10 9 8 7 6 5 4 3 2 1 WKT

Design by Jay Emmanuel
Lettering by Tess Stone

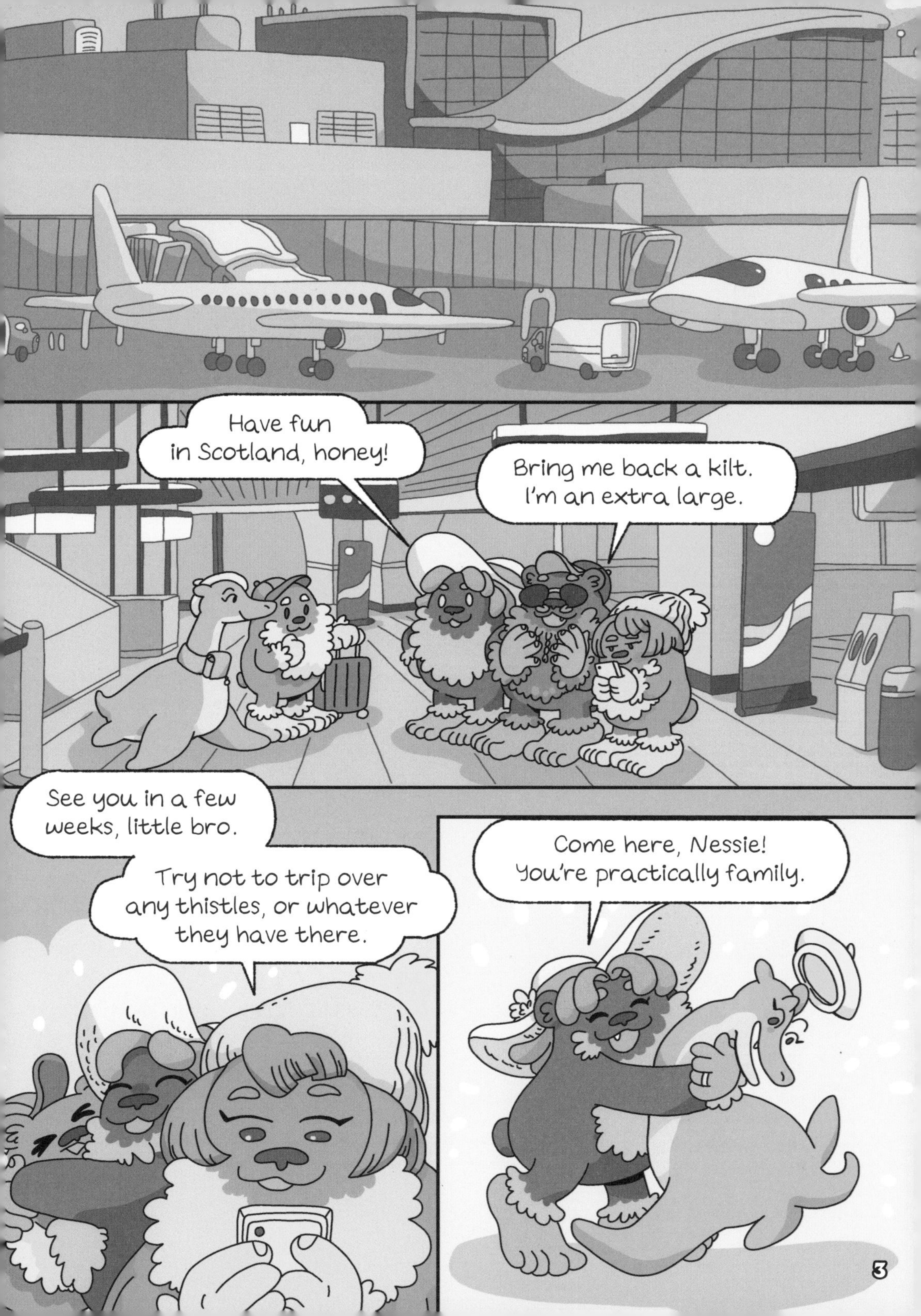

Have fun in Scotland, honey!
Bring me back a kilt. I'm an extra large.
See you in a few weeks, little bro.
Try not to trip over any thistles, or whatever they have there.
Come here, Nessie! You're practically family.

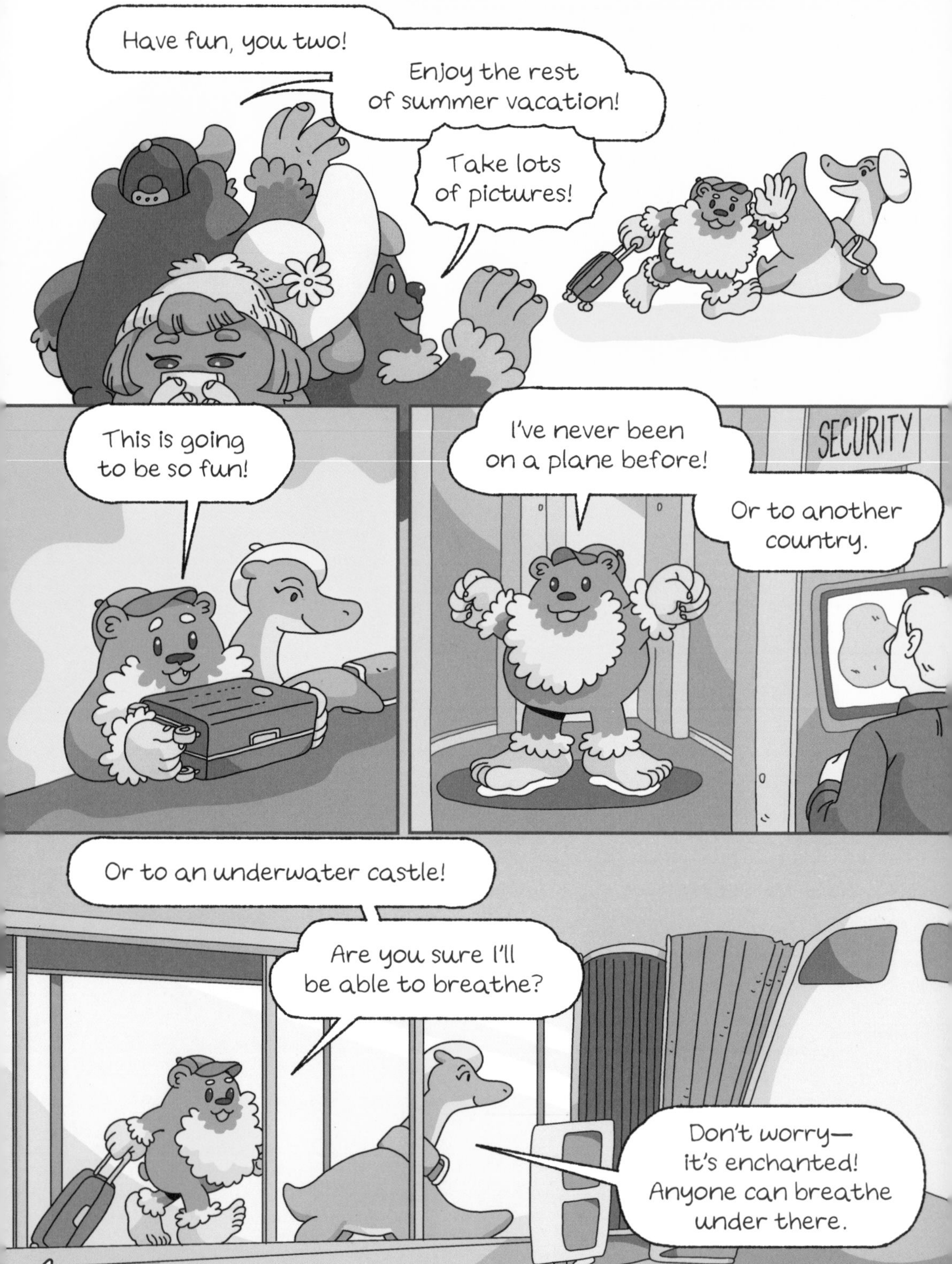

Have fun, you two!
Enjoy the rest of summer vacation!
Take lots of pictures!
This is going to be so fun!
I've never been on a plane before!
SECURITY
Or to another country.
Or to an underwater castle!
Are you sure I'll be able to breathe?
Don't worry—it's enchanted! Anyone can breathe under there.

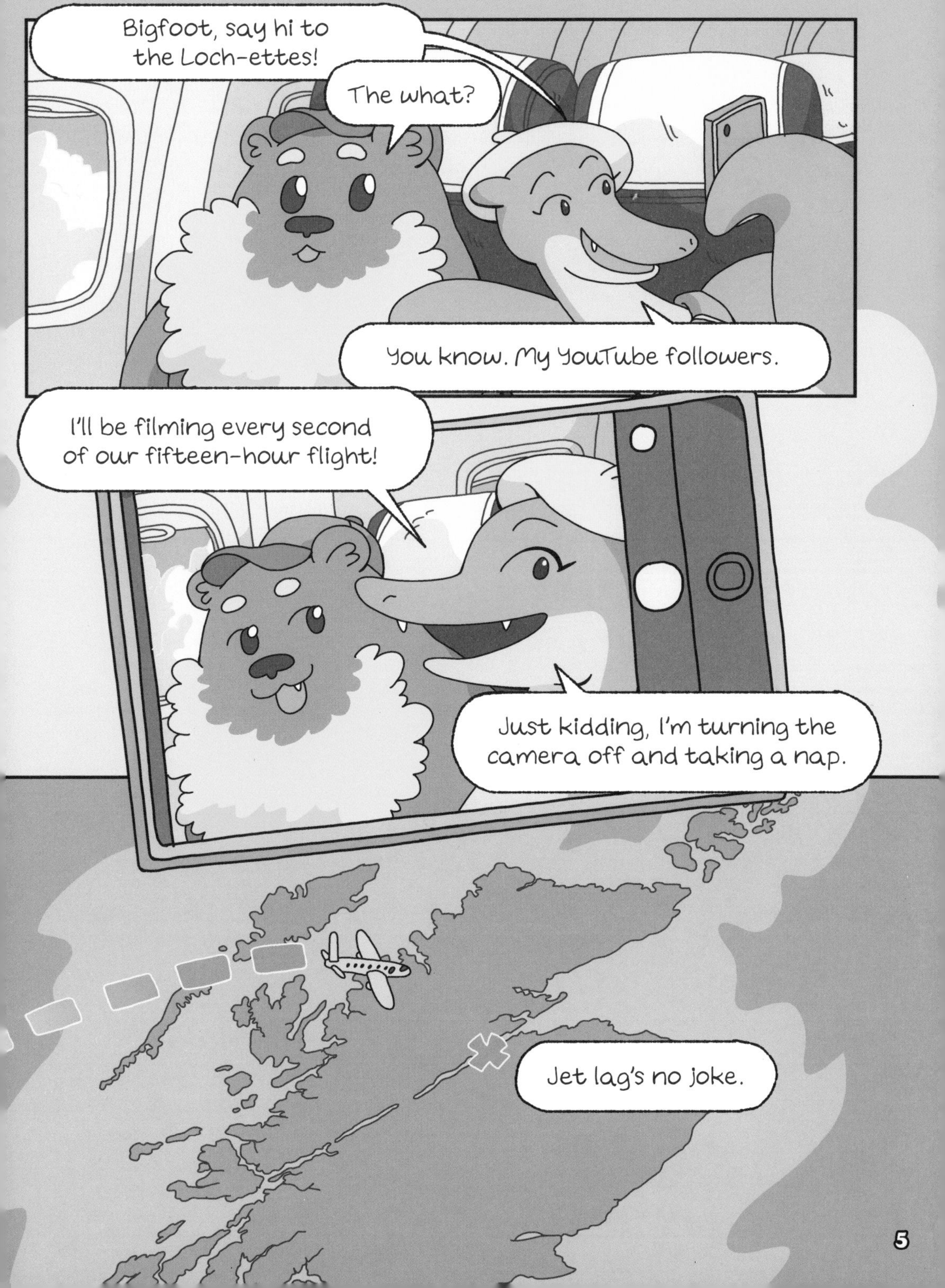
Bigfoot, say hi to the Loch-ettes!
The what?
You know. My YouTube followers.
I'll be filming every second of our fifteen-hour flight!
Just kidding, I'm turning the camera off and taking a nap.
Jet lag's no joke.

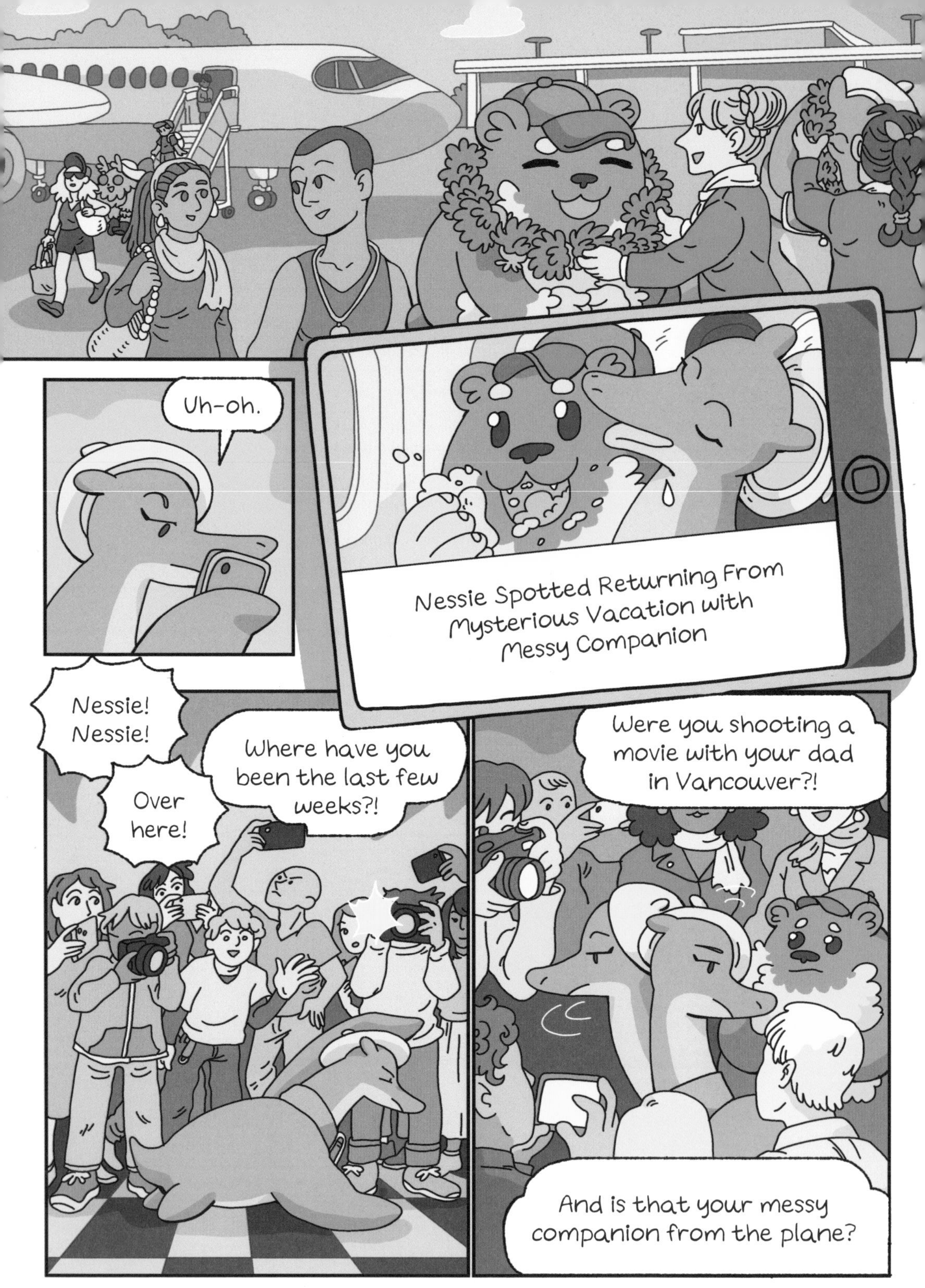
Uh-oh.
Nessie Spotted Returning From Mysterious Vacation with Messy Companion
Nessie! Nessie!
Over here!
Where have you been the last few weeks?!
Were you shooting a movie with your dad in Vancouver?!
And is that your messy companion from the plane?

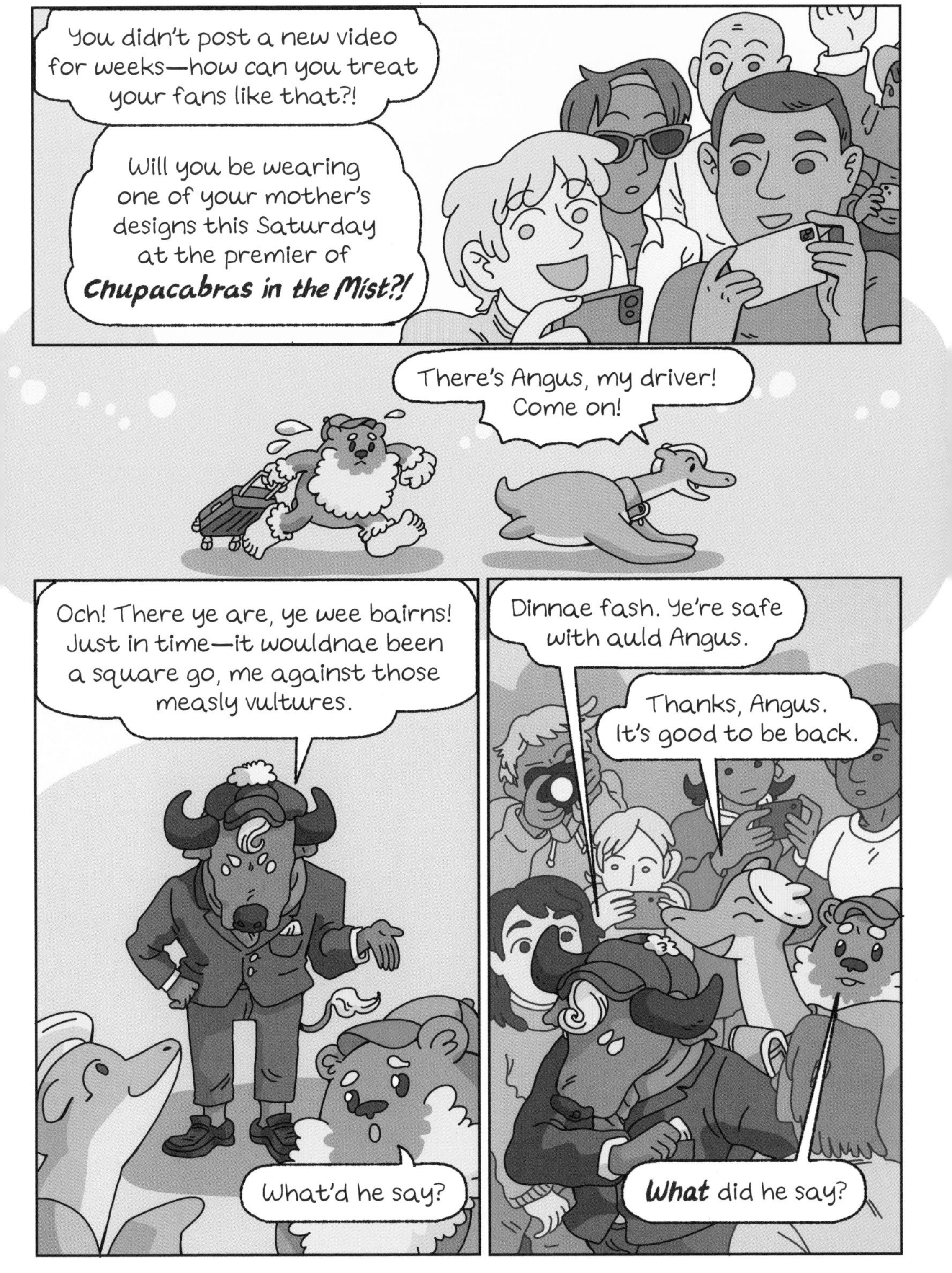
You didn't post a new video for weeks—how can you treat your fans like that?!
Will you be wearing one of your mother's designs this Saturday at the premier of **Chupacabras in the Mist?!**
There's Angus, my driver! Come on!
Och! There ye are, ye wee bairns! Just in time—it wouldnae been a square go, me against those measly vultures.
What'd he say?
Dinnae fash. Ye're safe with auld Angus.
Thanks, Angus. It's good to be back.
What did he say?

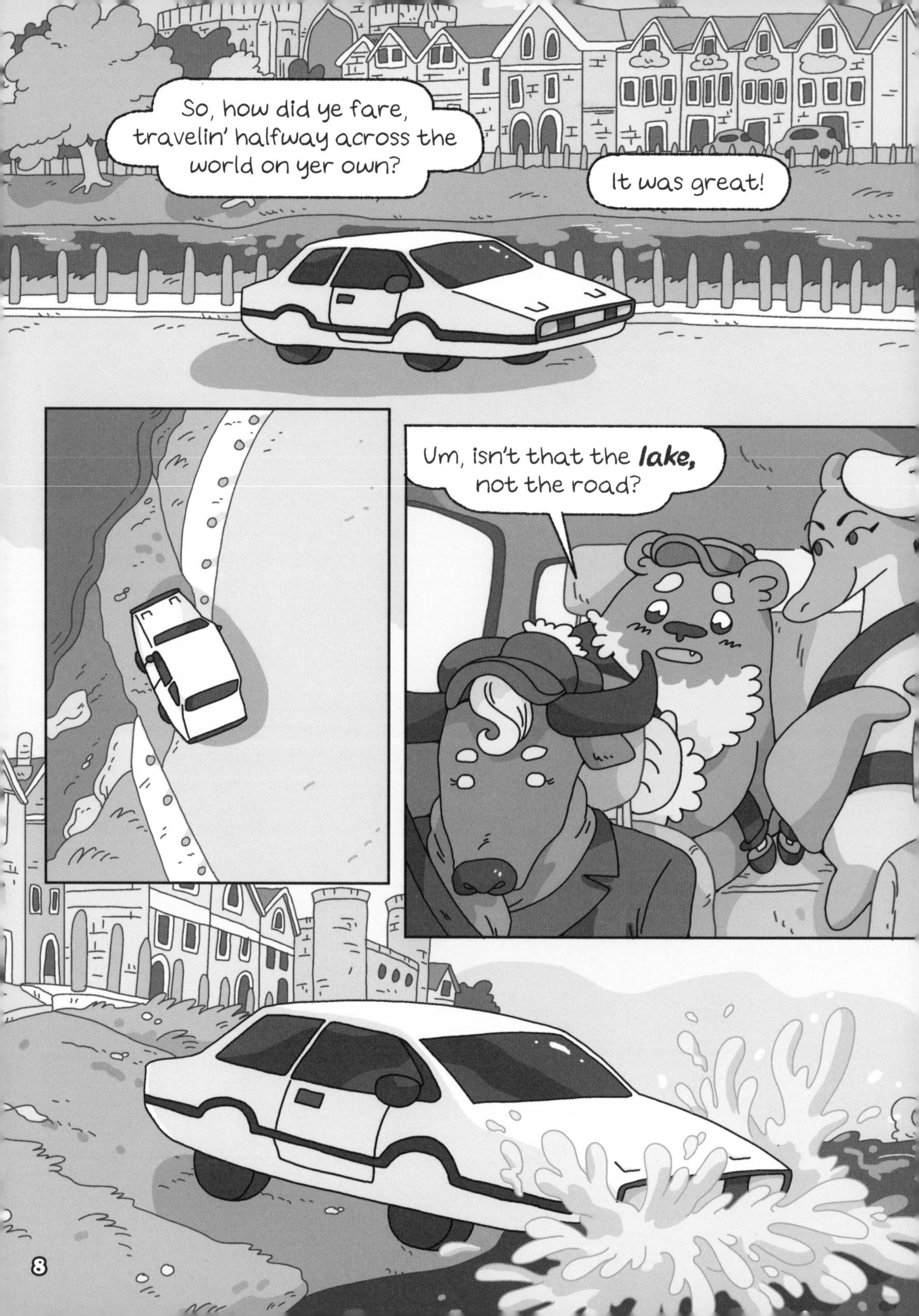
So, how did ye fare, travelin' halfway across the world on yer own?
It was great!
Um, isn't that the **lake,** not the road?

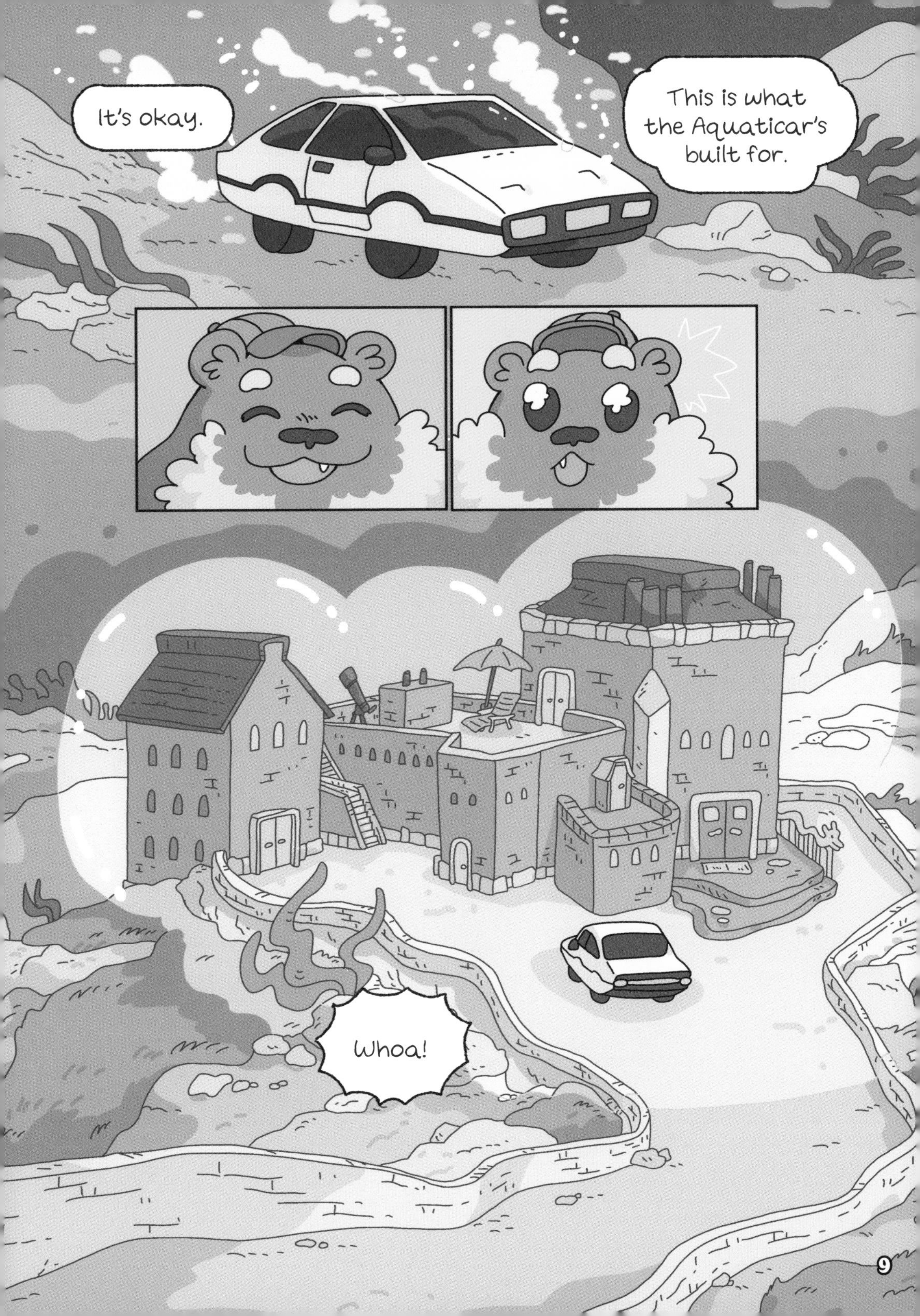
It's okay.
This is what the Aquaticar's built for.
Whoa!

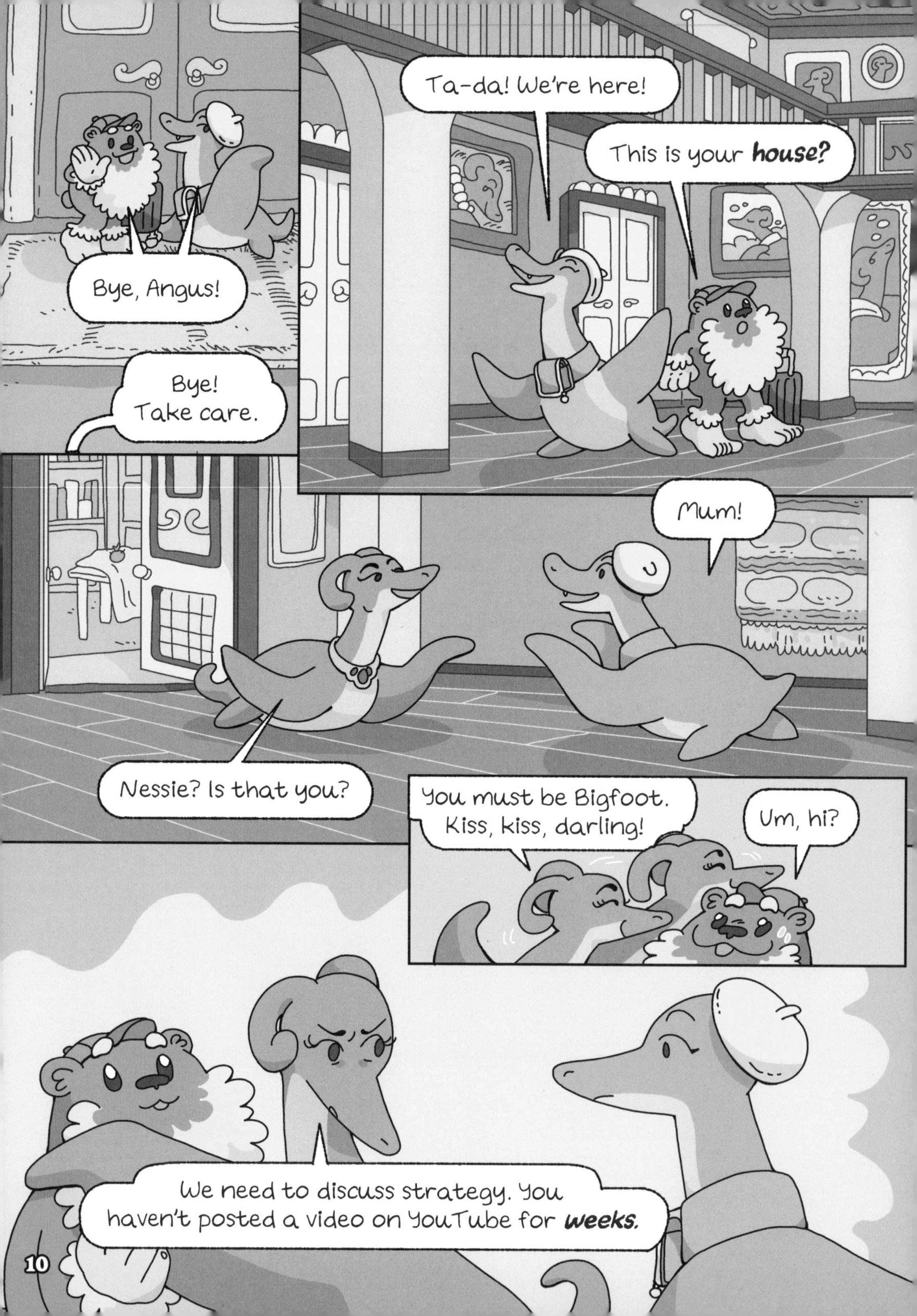
Bye, Angus!
Bye! Take care.
Ta-da! We're here!
This is your **house?**
Mum!
Nessie? Is that you?
You must be Bigfoot. Kiss, kiss, darling!
Um, hi?
We need to discuss strategy. You haven't posted a video on YouTube for ***weeks.***

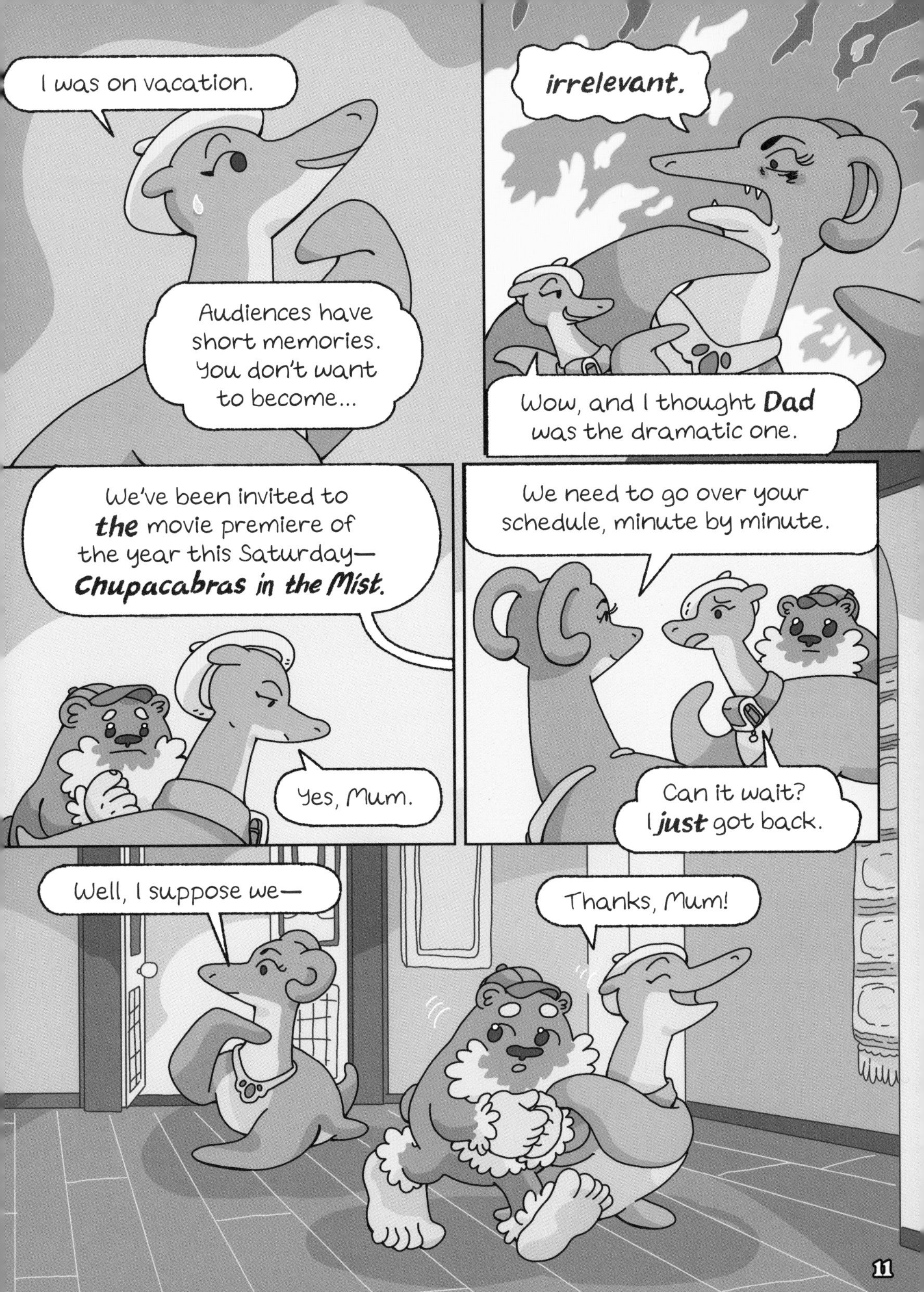
I was on vacation.
Audiences have short memories. You don't want to become...
irrelevant.
Wow, and I thought Dad was the dramatic one.
We've been invited to the movie premiere of the year this Saturday—Chupacabras in the Mist.
Yes, Mum.
We need to go over your schedule, minute by minute.
Can it wait? I just got back.
Well, I suppose we—
Thanks, Mum!

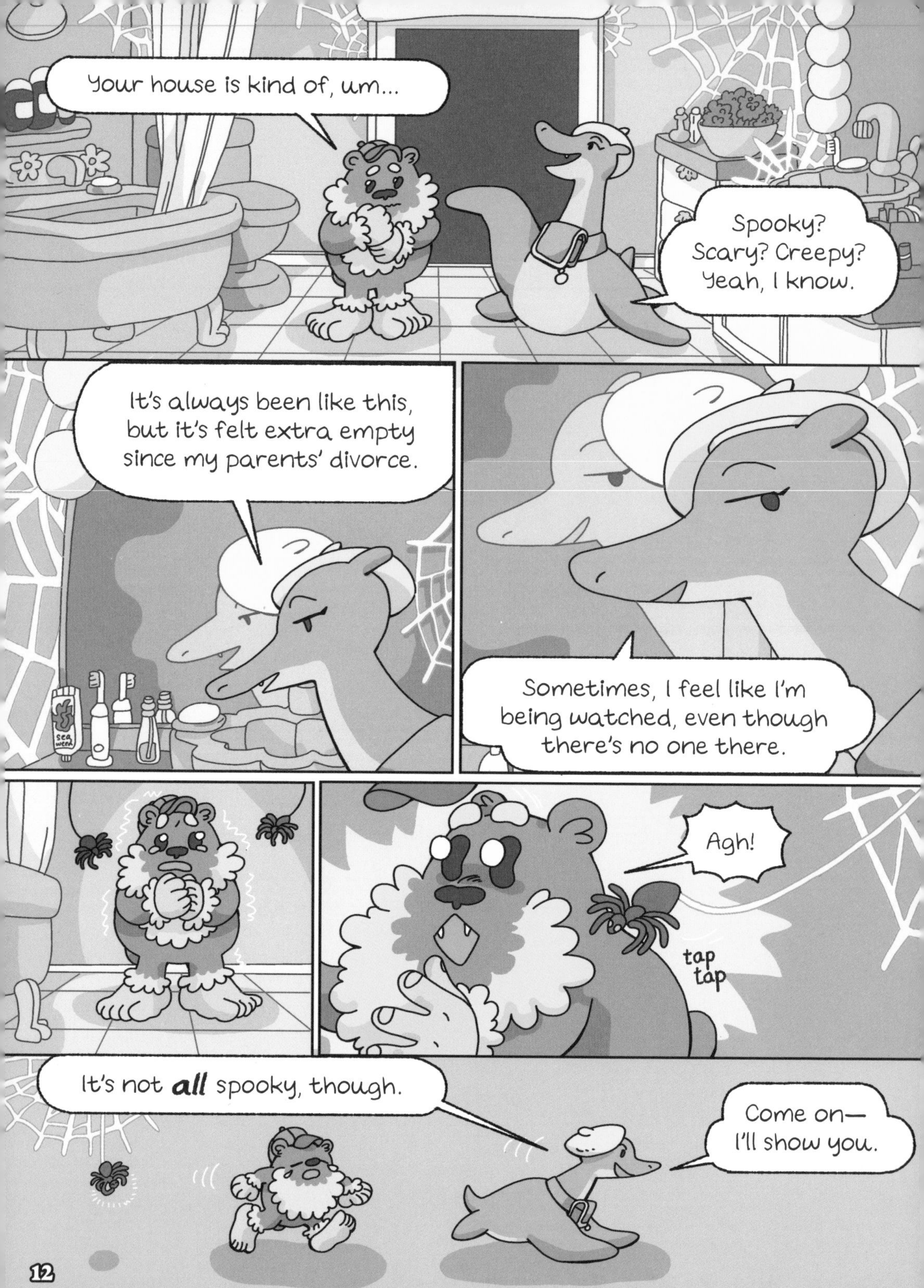
Your house is kind of, um...
Spooky? Scary? Creepy? Yeah, I know.
It's always been like this, but it's felt extra empty since my parents' divorce.
sea weed
Sometimes, I feel like I'm being watched, even though there's no one there.
Agh!
tap tap
It's not **all** spooky, though.
Come on— I'll show you.

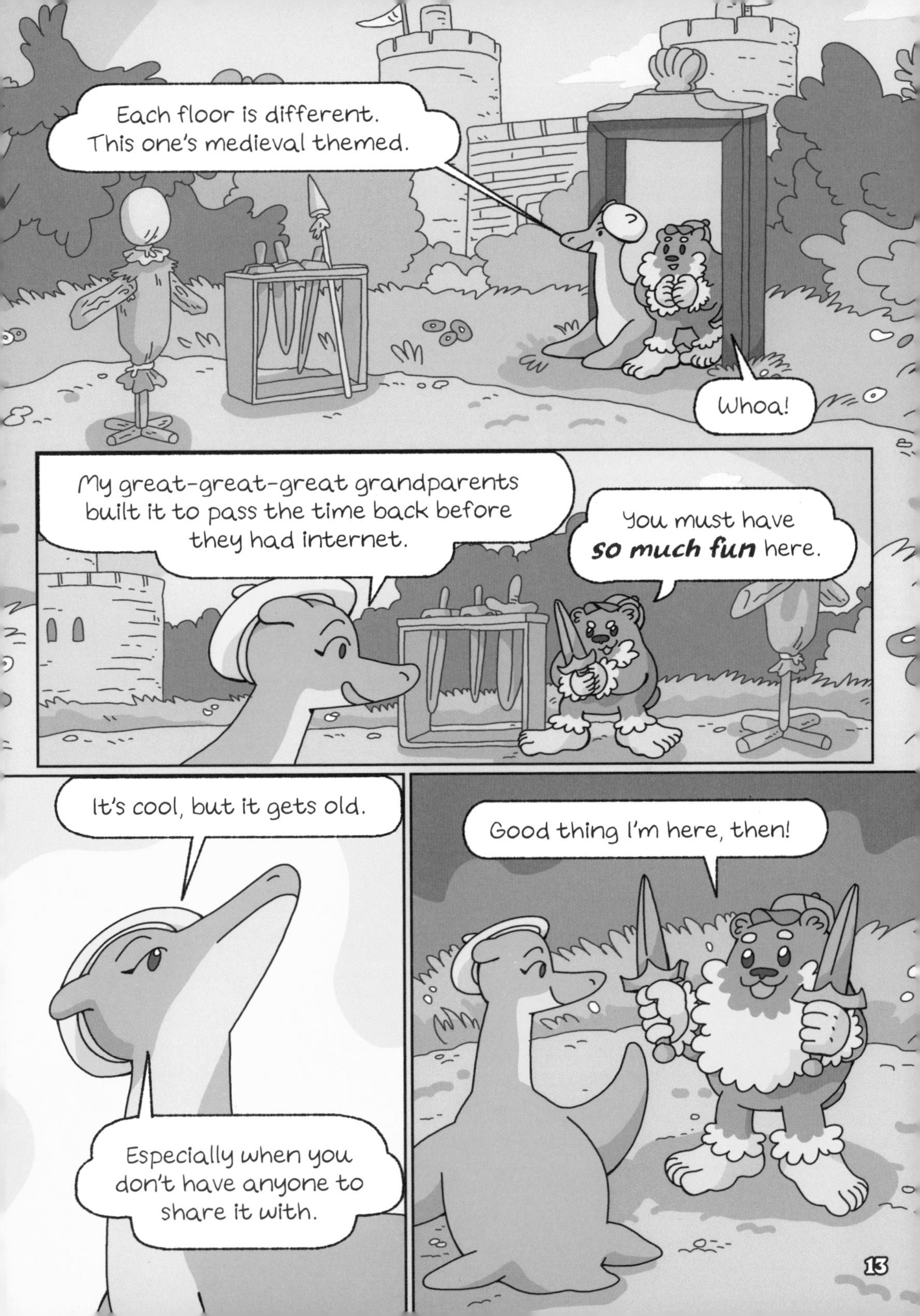
Each floor is different. This one's medieval themed.
Whoa!
My great-great-great grandparents built it to pass the time back before they had internet.
You must have **so much fun** here.
It's cool, but it gets old.
Especially when you don't have anyone to share it with.
Good thing I'm here, then!

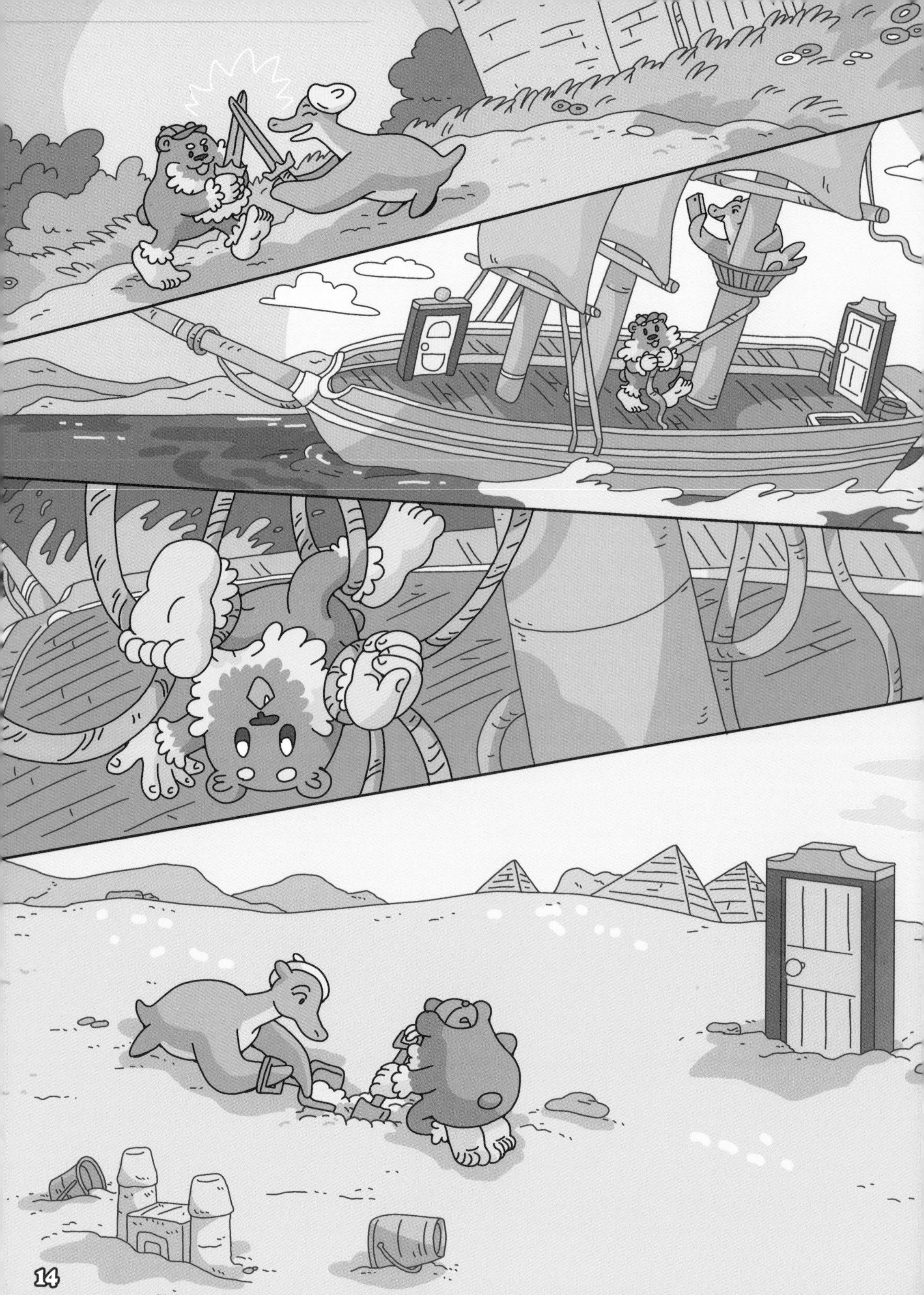

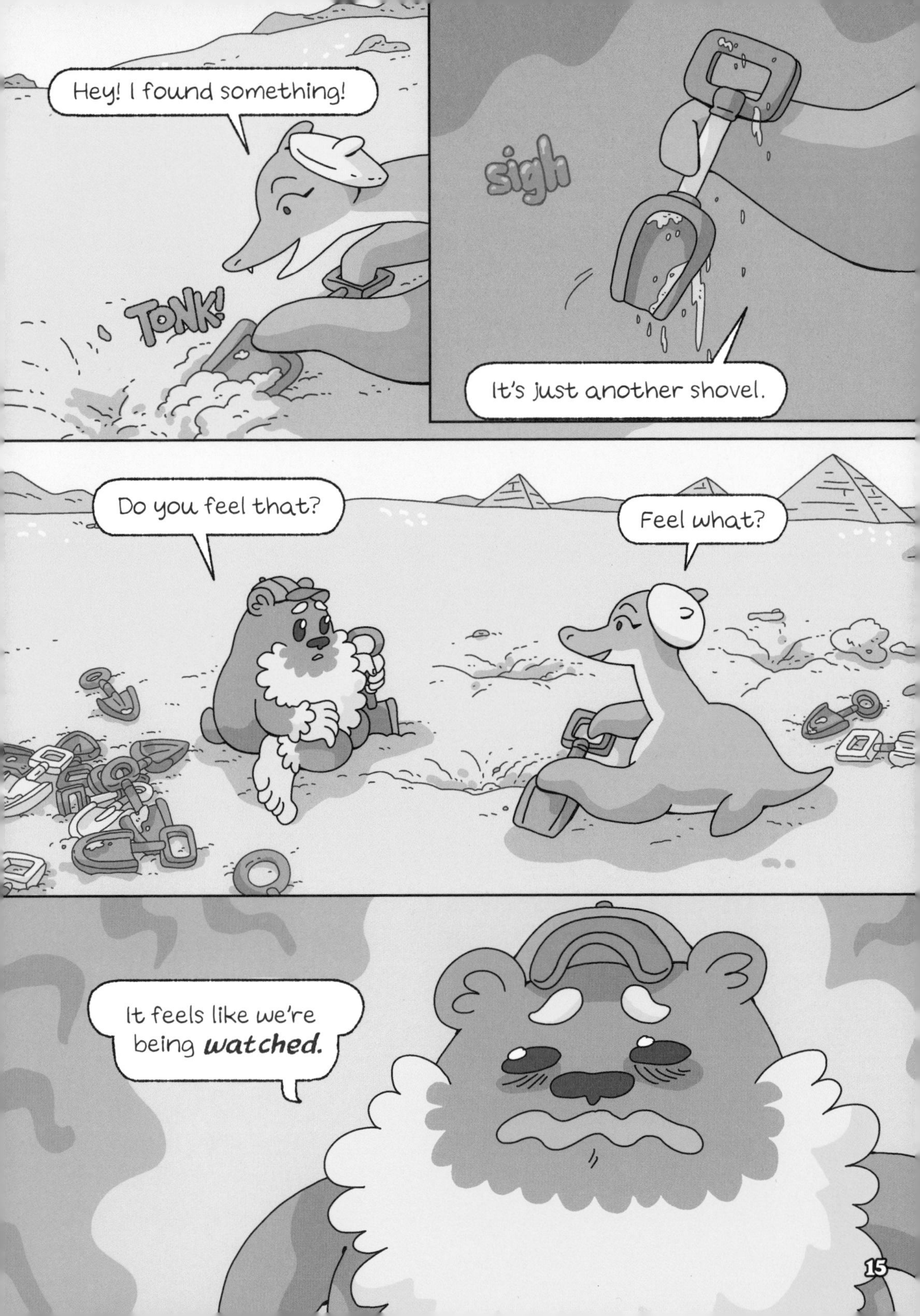
Hey! I found something!
TONK!
sigh
It's just another shovel.
Do you feel that?
Feel what?
It feels like we're being ***watched.***

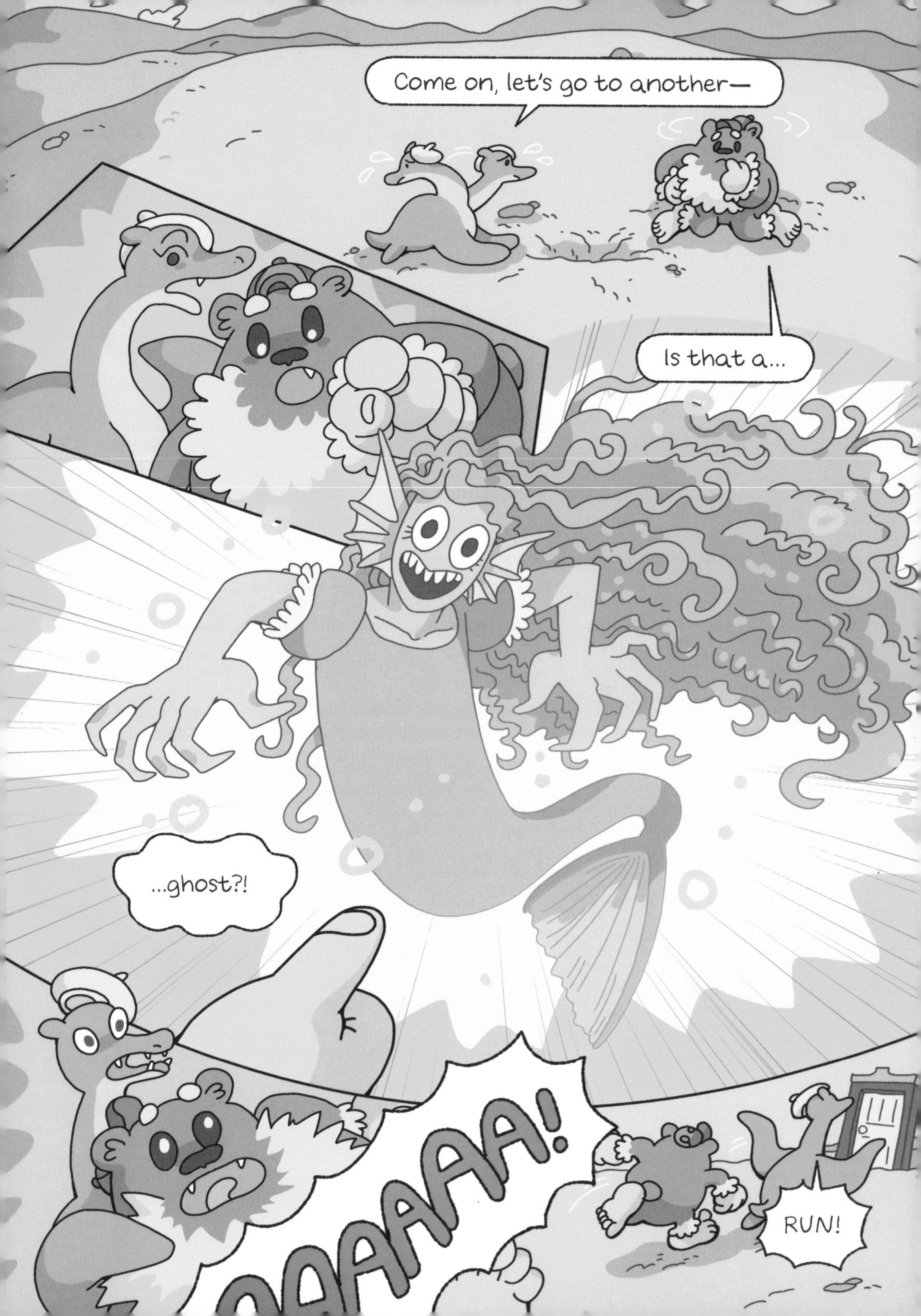
Come on, let's go to another—
Is that a...
...ghost?!
AAAAAAAA!
RUN!

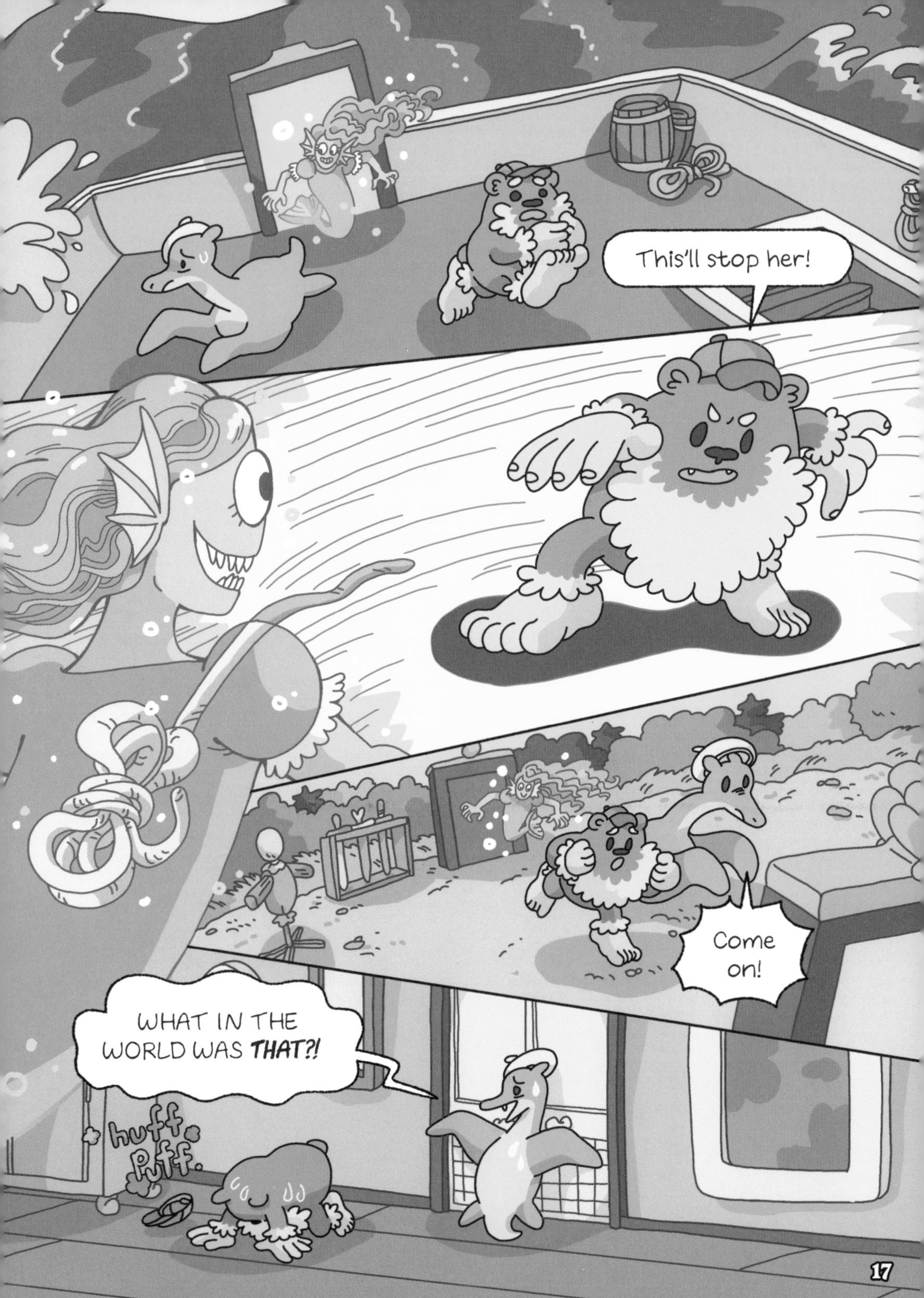
This'll stop her!
Come on!
WHAT IN THE WORLD WAS **THAT?!**
huff
puff.

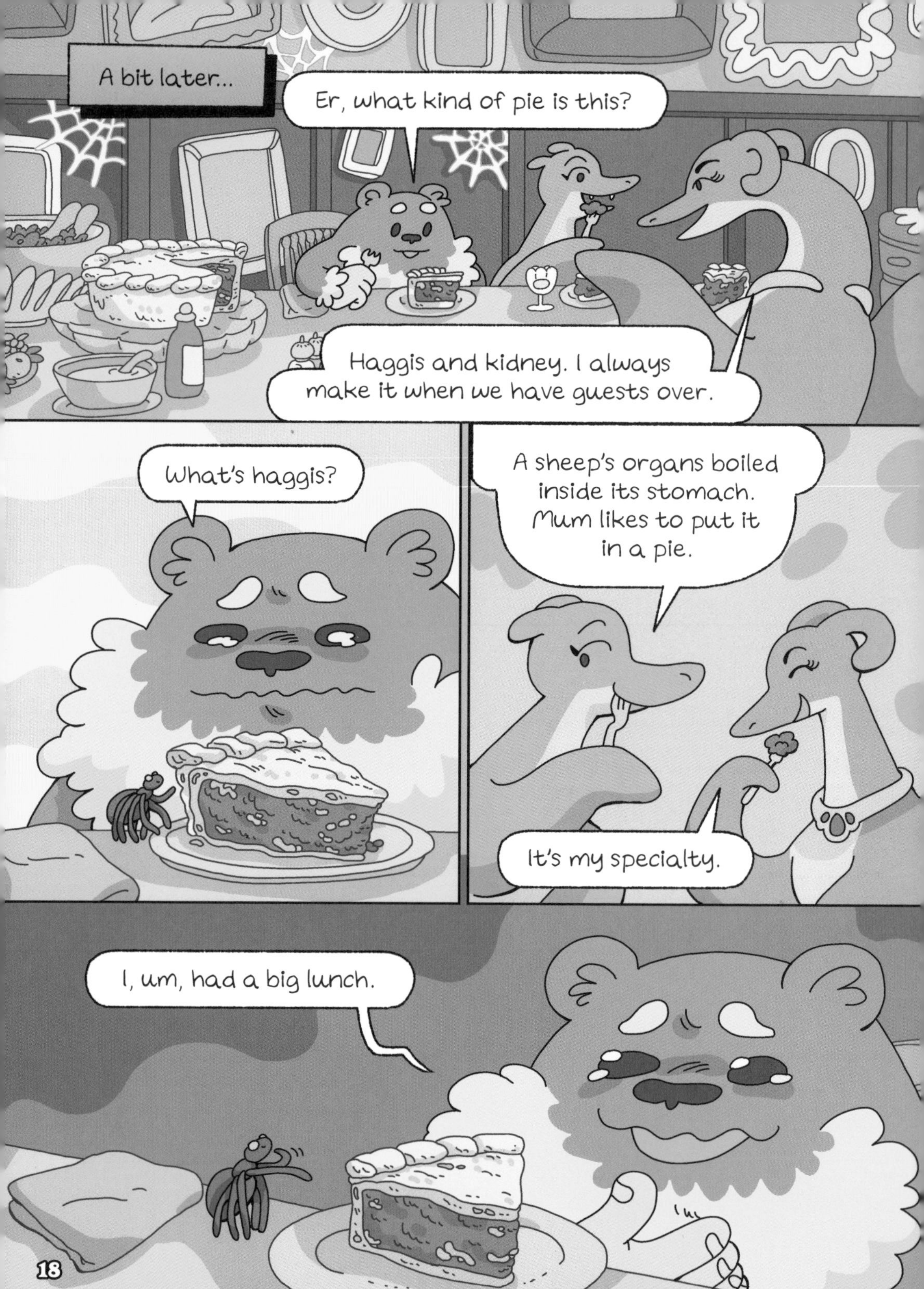
A bit later...
Er, what kind of pie is this?
Haggis and kidney. I always make it when we have guests over.
What's haggis?
A sheep's organs boiled inside its stomach. Mum likes to put it in a pie.
It's my specialty.
I, um, had a big lunch.

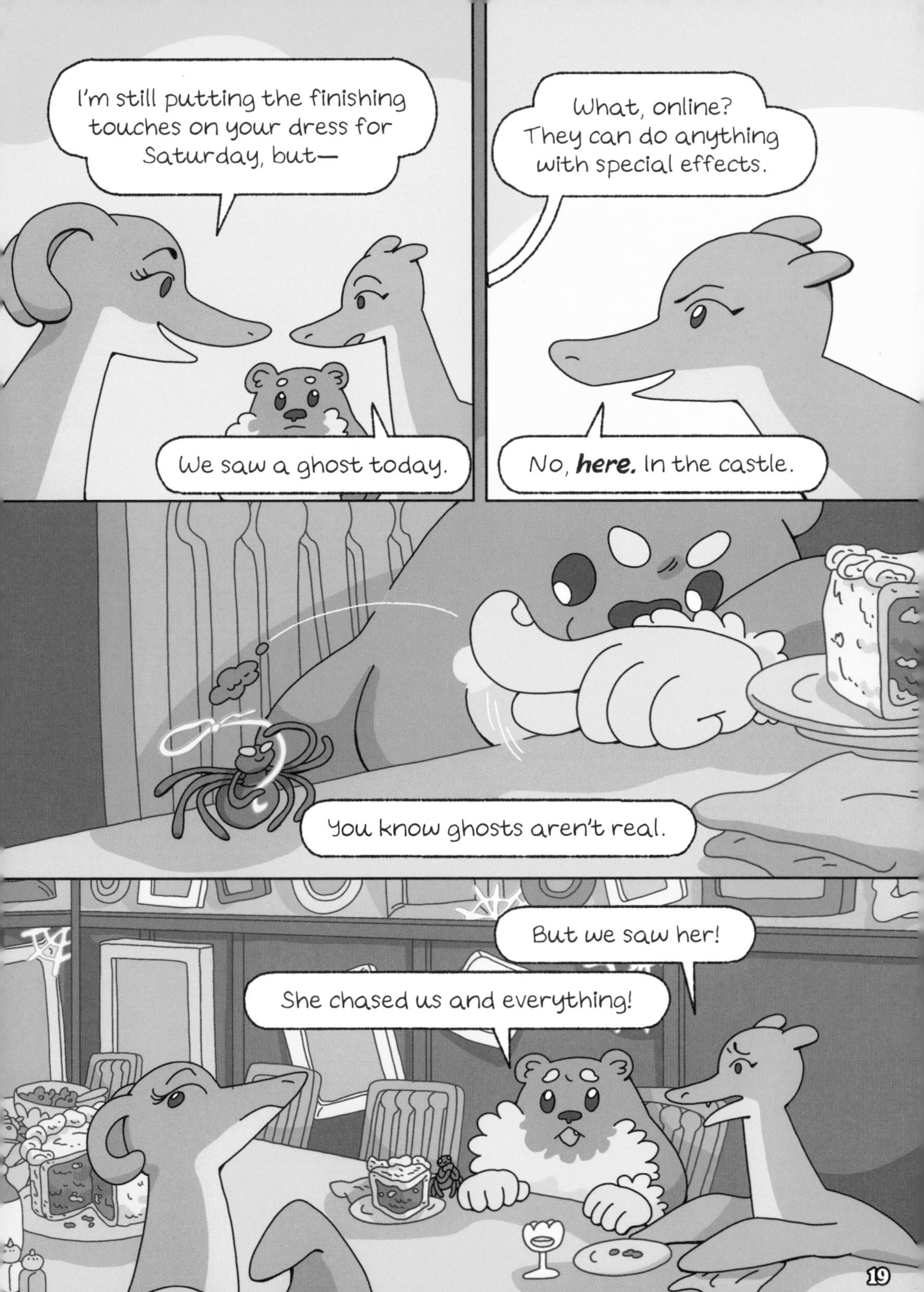
I'm still putting the finishing touches on your dress for Saturday, but—
We saw a ghost today.
What, online? They can do anything with special effects.
No, **here.** In the castle.
You know ghosts aren't real.
But we saw her!
She chased us and everything!

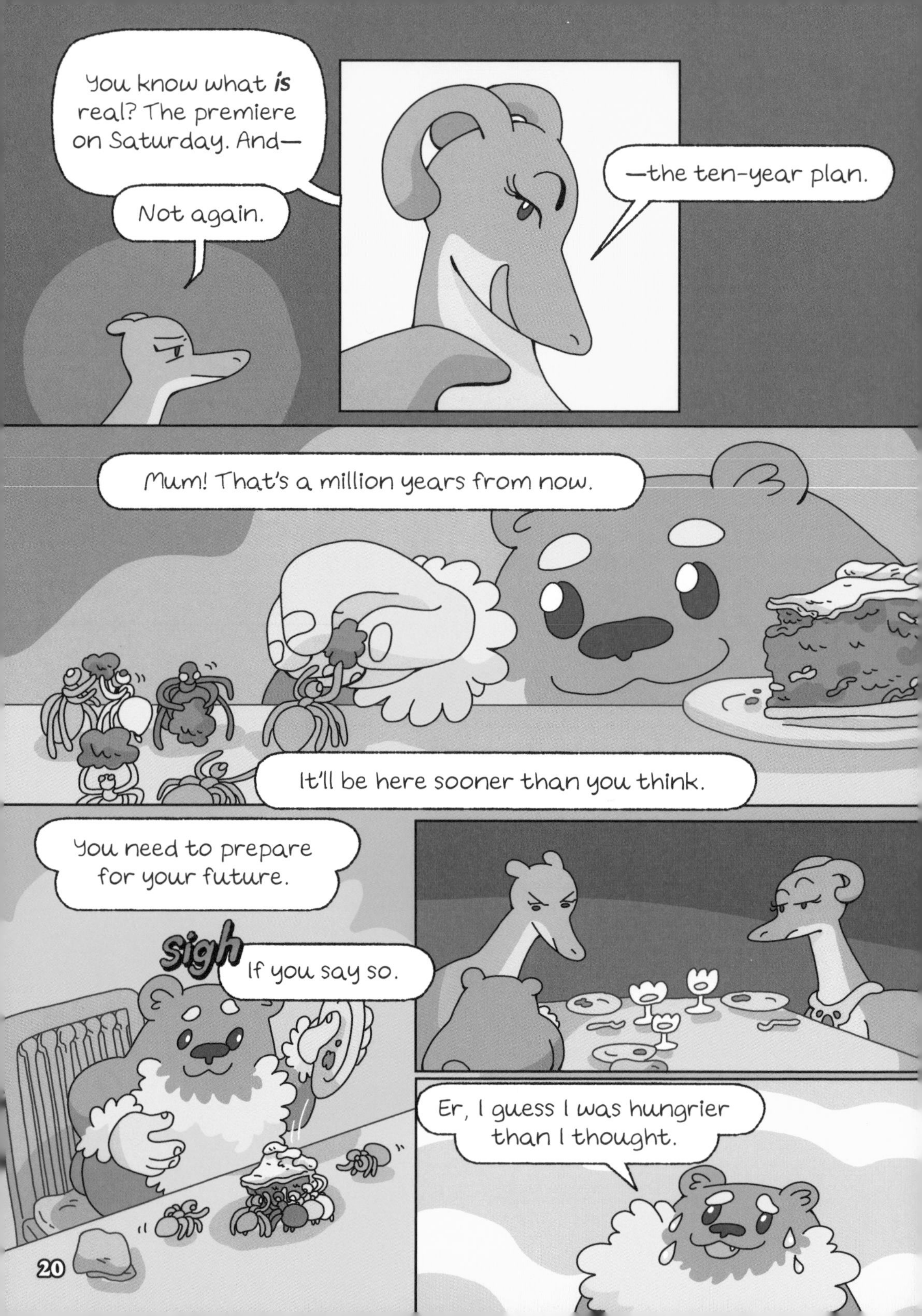
You know what **is** real? The premiere on Saturday. And—
Not again.
—the ten-year plan.
Mum! That's a million years from now.
It'll be here sooner than you think.
You need to prepare for your future.
sigh
If you say so.
Er, I guess I was hungrier than I thought.

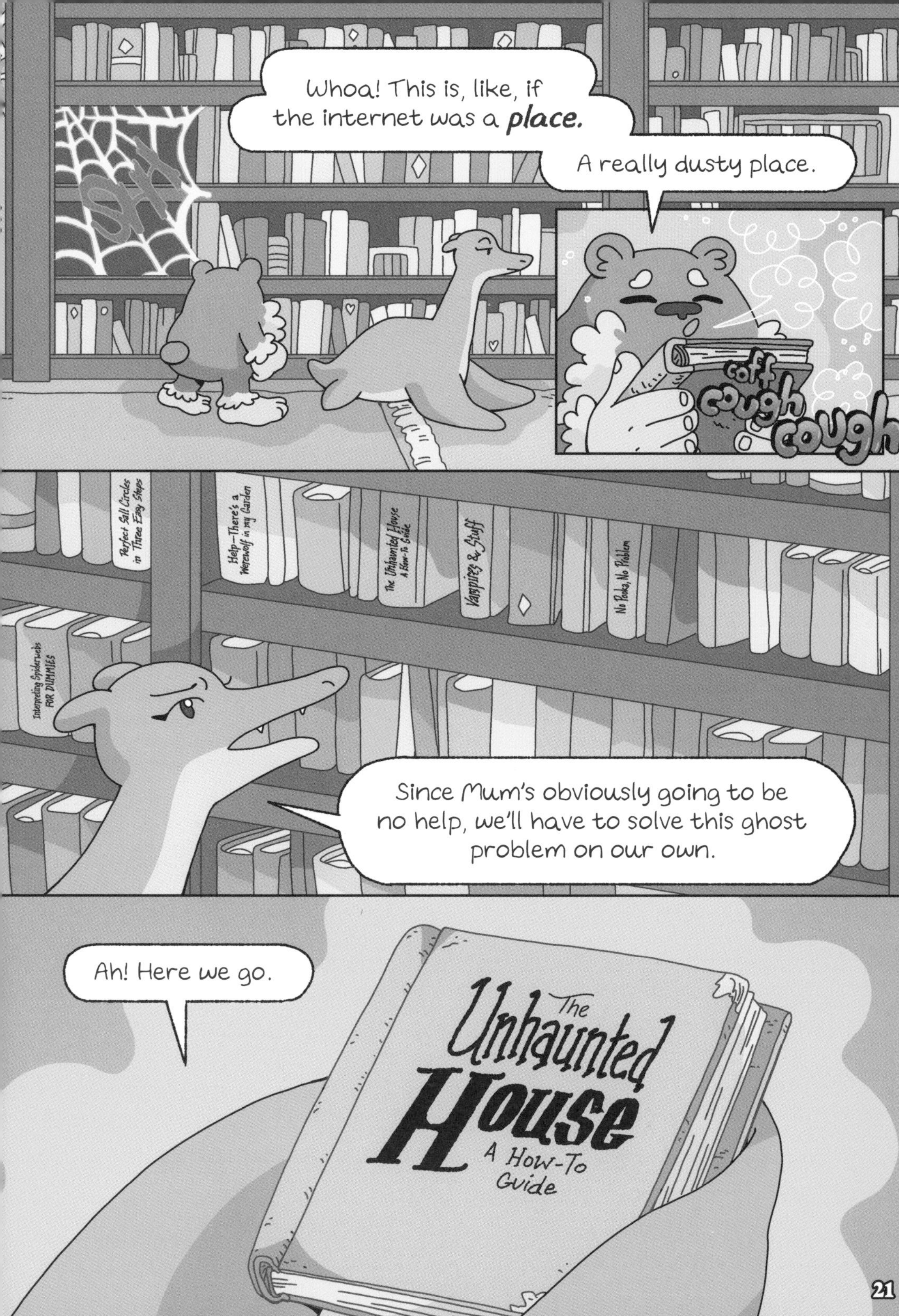

Whoa! This is, like, if the internet was a ***place.***
SHH
A really dusty place.
coff cough cough
Perfect Salt Circles in Three Easy Steps
Help—There's a Werewolf in my Garden
The Unhaunted House A How-To Guide
Vampires & Stuff
No Pooka, No Problem
Interpreting Spiderwebs FOR DUMMIES
Since Mum's obviously going to be no help, we'll have to solve this ghost problem on our own.
Ah! Here we go.
The Unhaunted House A How-To Guide

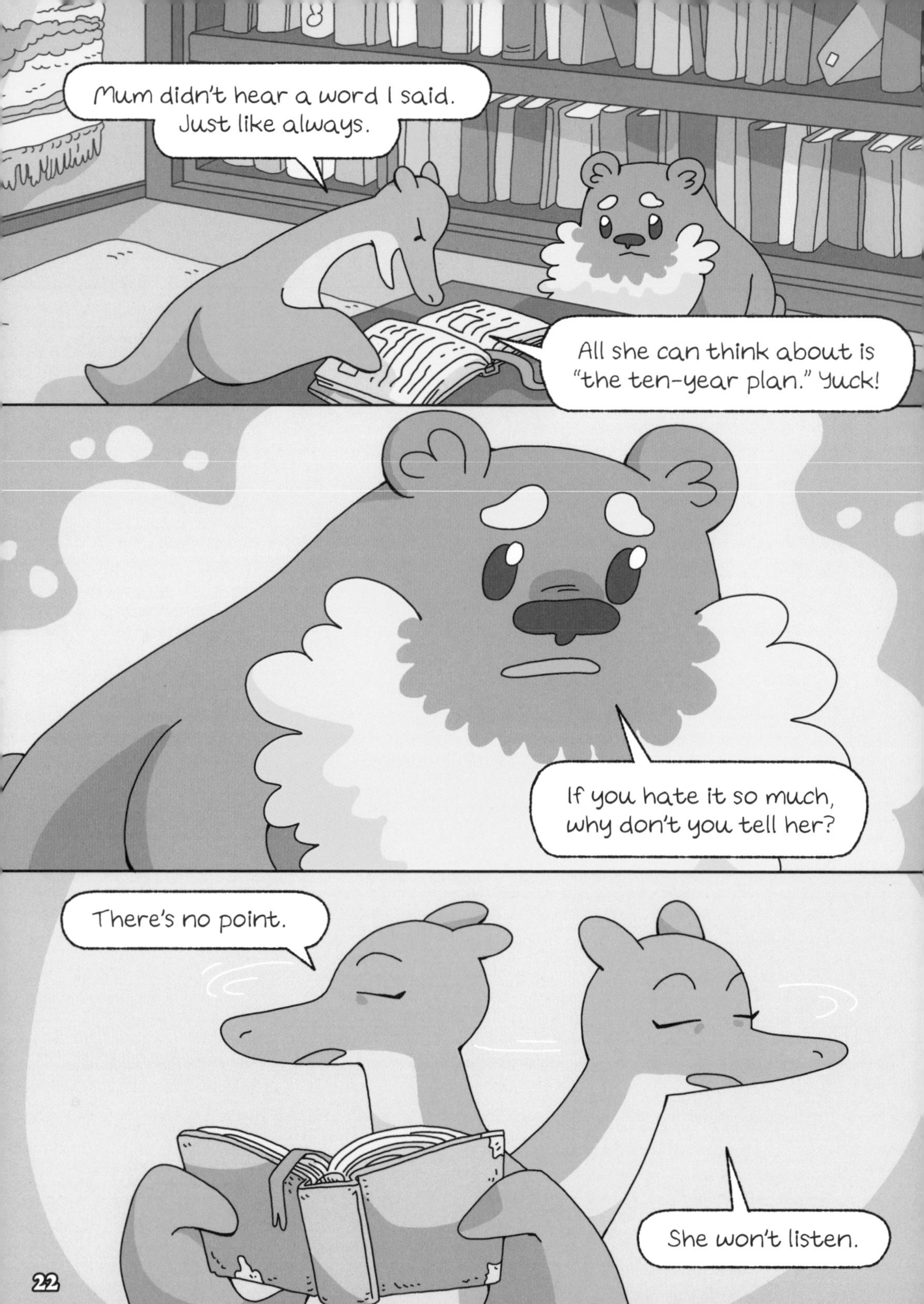
Mum didn't hear a word I said. Just like always.
All she can think about is "the ten-year plan." Yuck!
If you hate it so much, why don't you tell her?
There's no point.
She won't listen.

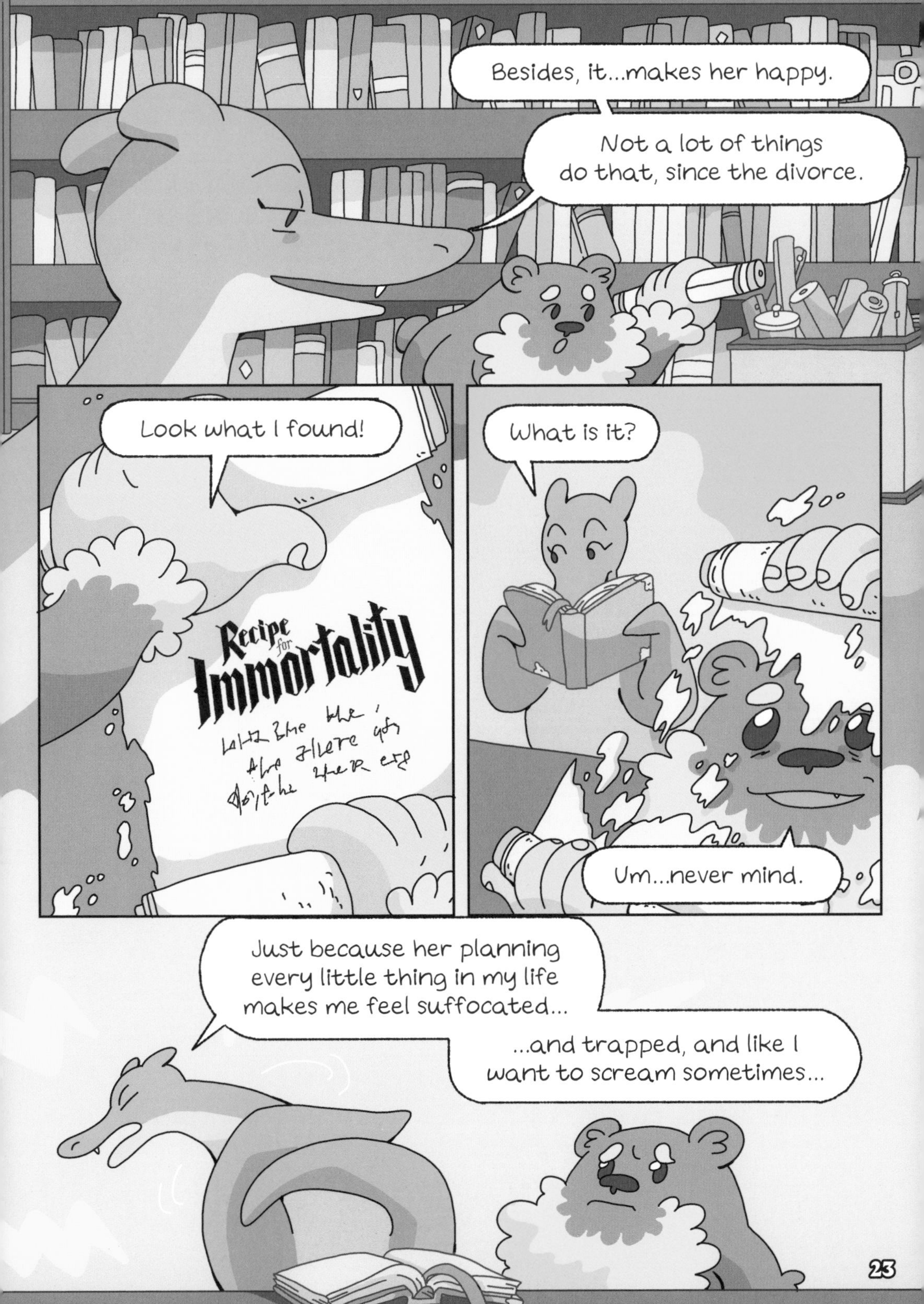
Besides, it...makes her happy.
Not a lot of things do that, since the divorce.
Look what I found!
Recipe for Immortality
What is it?
Um...never mind.
Just because her planning every little thing in my life makes me feel suffocated...
...and trapped, and like I want to scream sometimes...

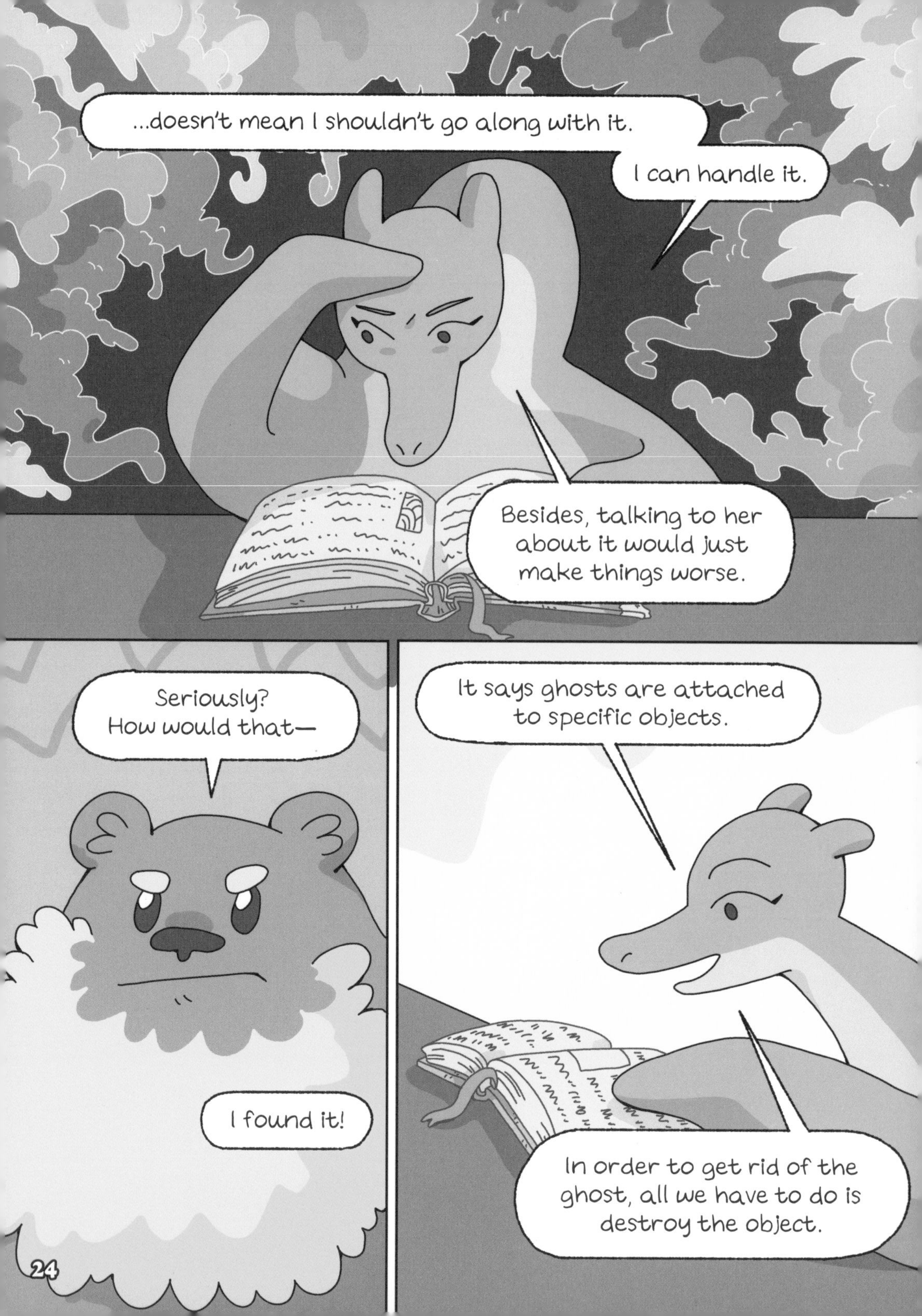
...doesn't mean I shouldn't go along with it.
I can handle it.
Besides, talking to her about it would just make things worse.
Seriously? How would that—
I found it!
It says ghosts are attached to specific objects.
In order to get rid of the ghost, all we have to do is destroy the object.

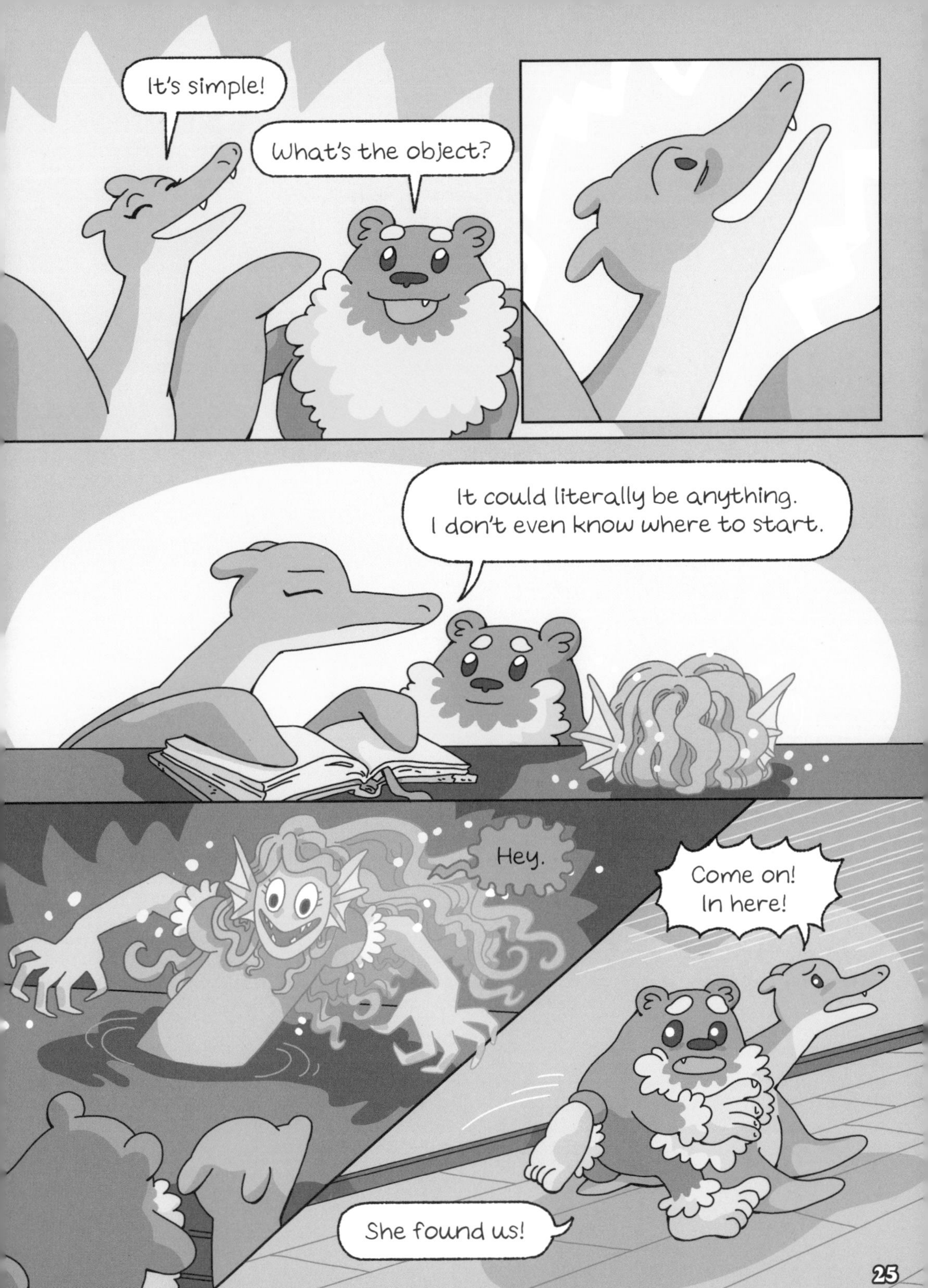
It's simple!
What's the object?
It could literally be anything. I don't even know where to start.
Hey.
Come on! In here!
She found us!

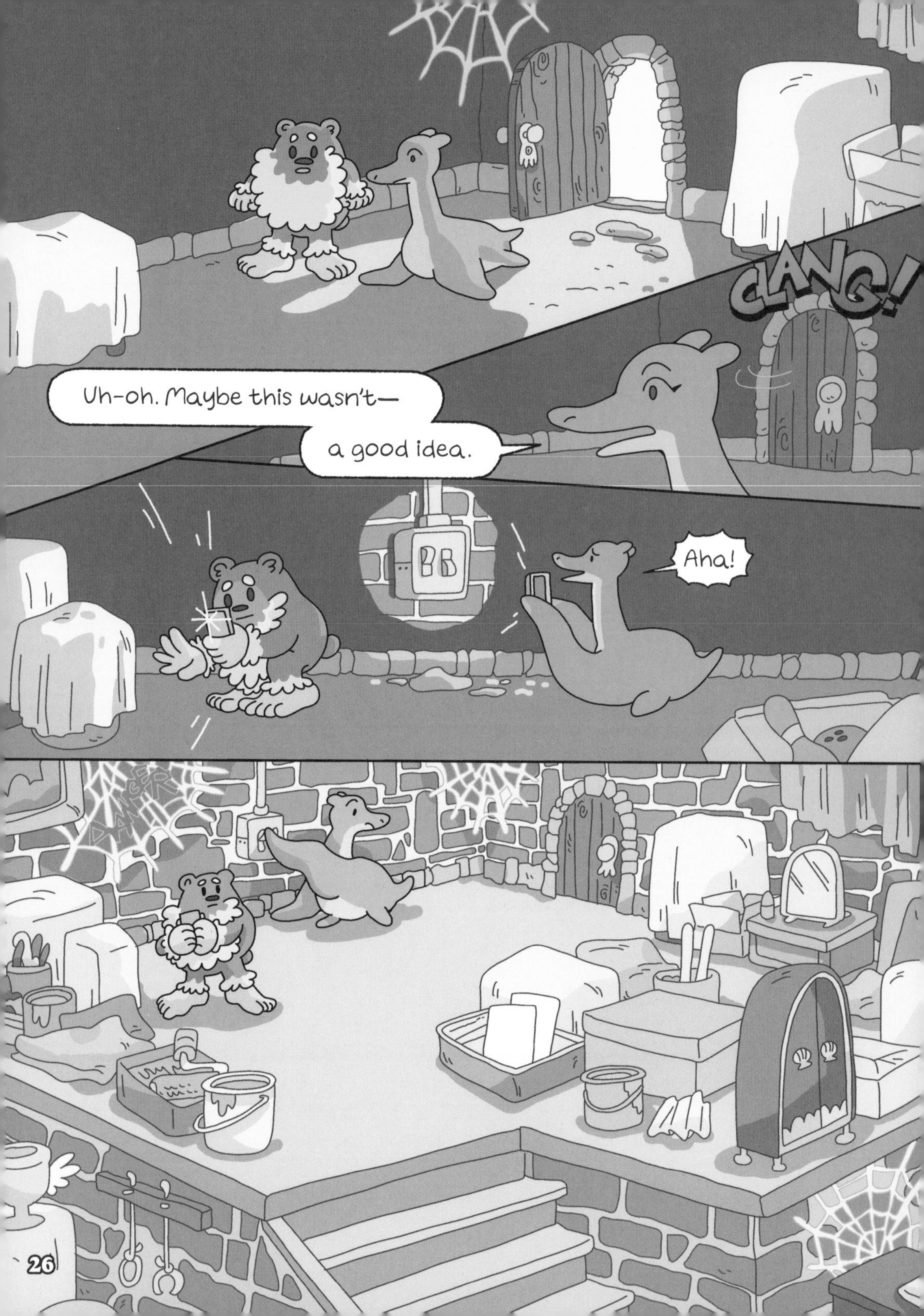
CLANG!
Uh-oh. Maybe this wasn't—
a good idea.
Aha!

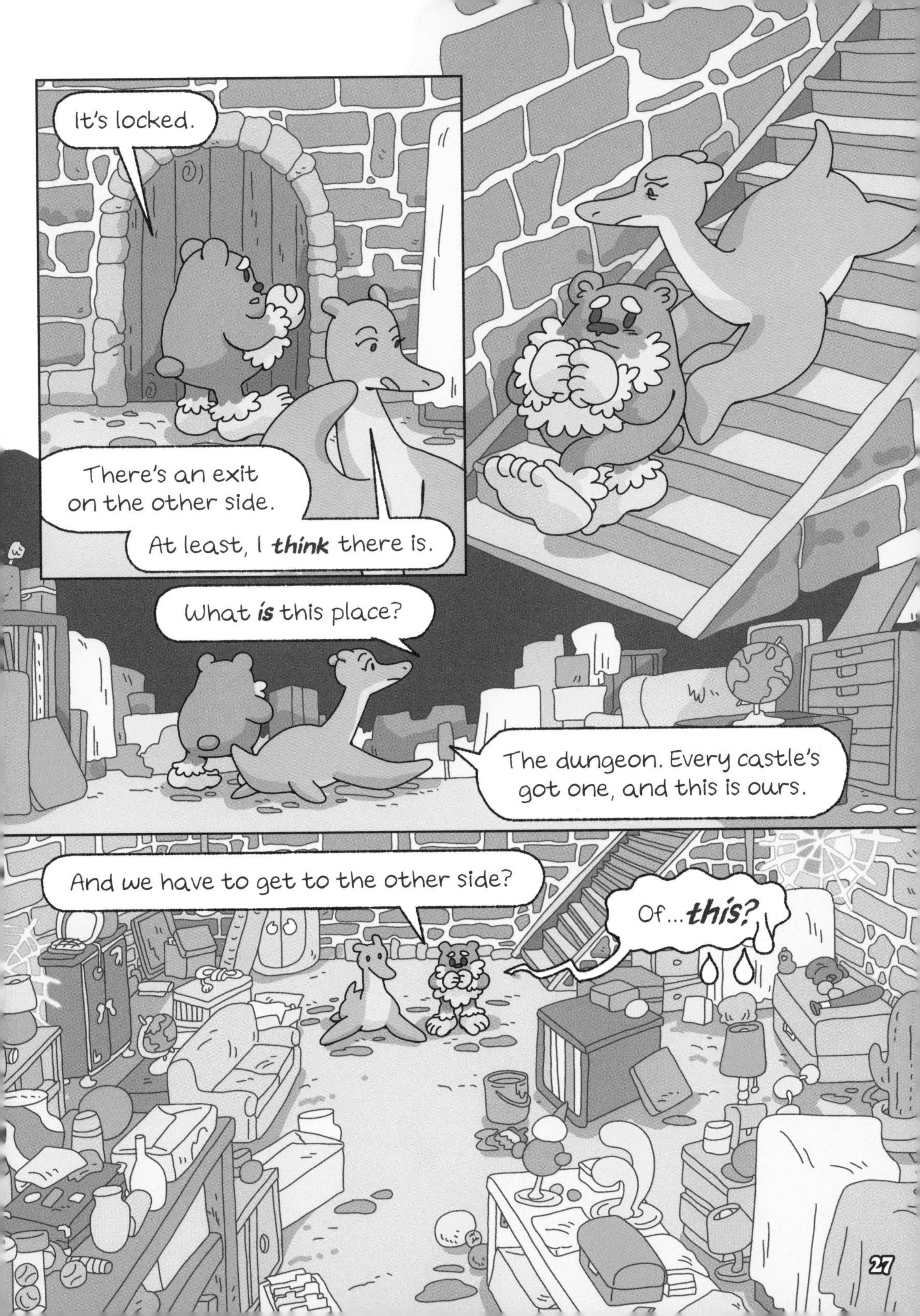
It's locked.
There's an exit on the other side.
At least, I **think** there is.
What **is** this place?
The dungeon. Every castle's got one, and this is ours.
And we have to get to the other side?
Of... **this?**

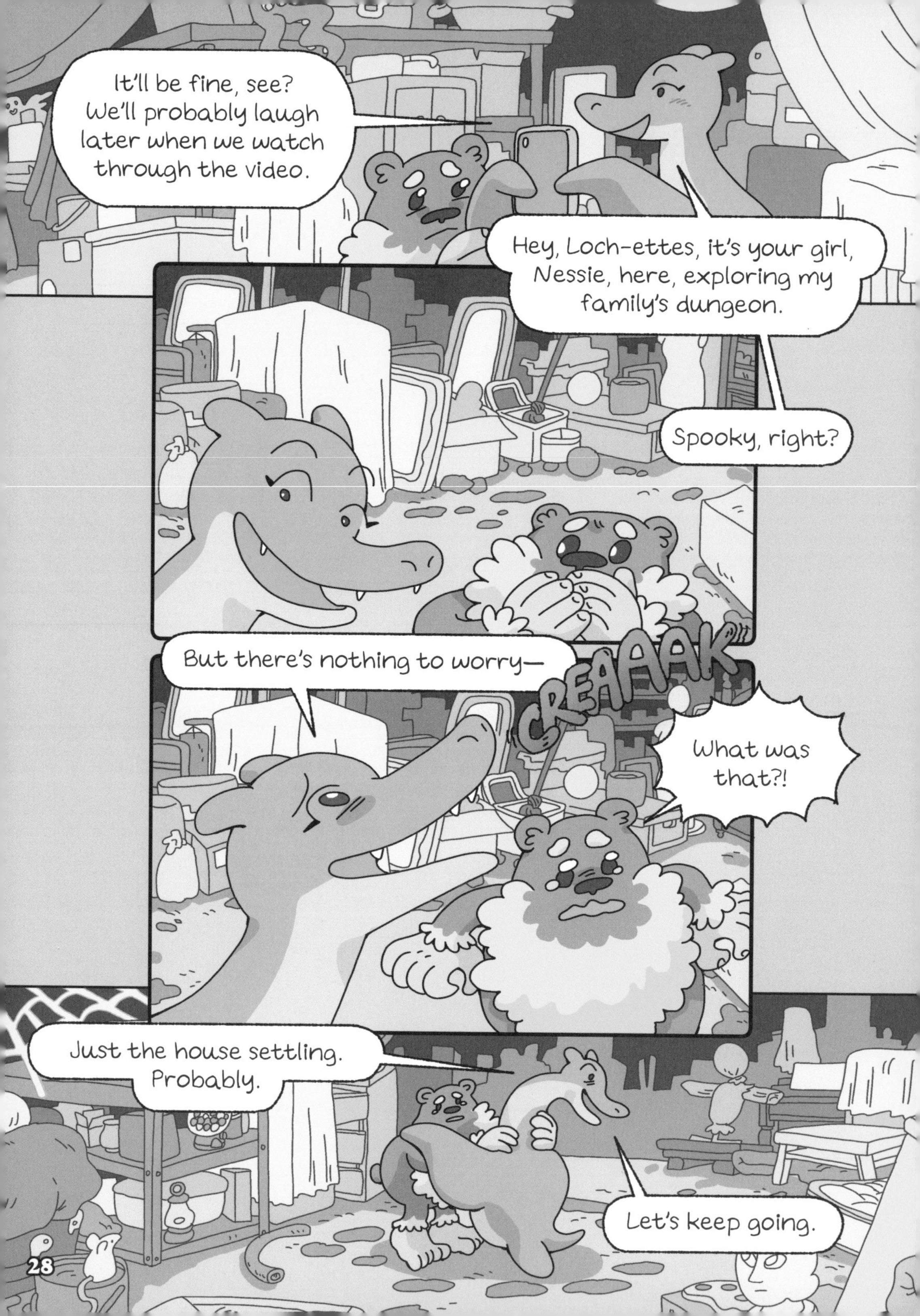

It'll be fine, see? We'll probably laugh later when we watch through the video.
Hey, Loch-ettes, it's your girl, Nessie, here, exploring my family's dungeon.
Spooky, right?
But there's nothing to worry—
CREAAAK
What was that?!
Just the house settling. Probably.
Let's keep going.

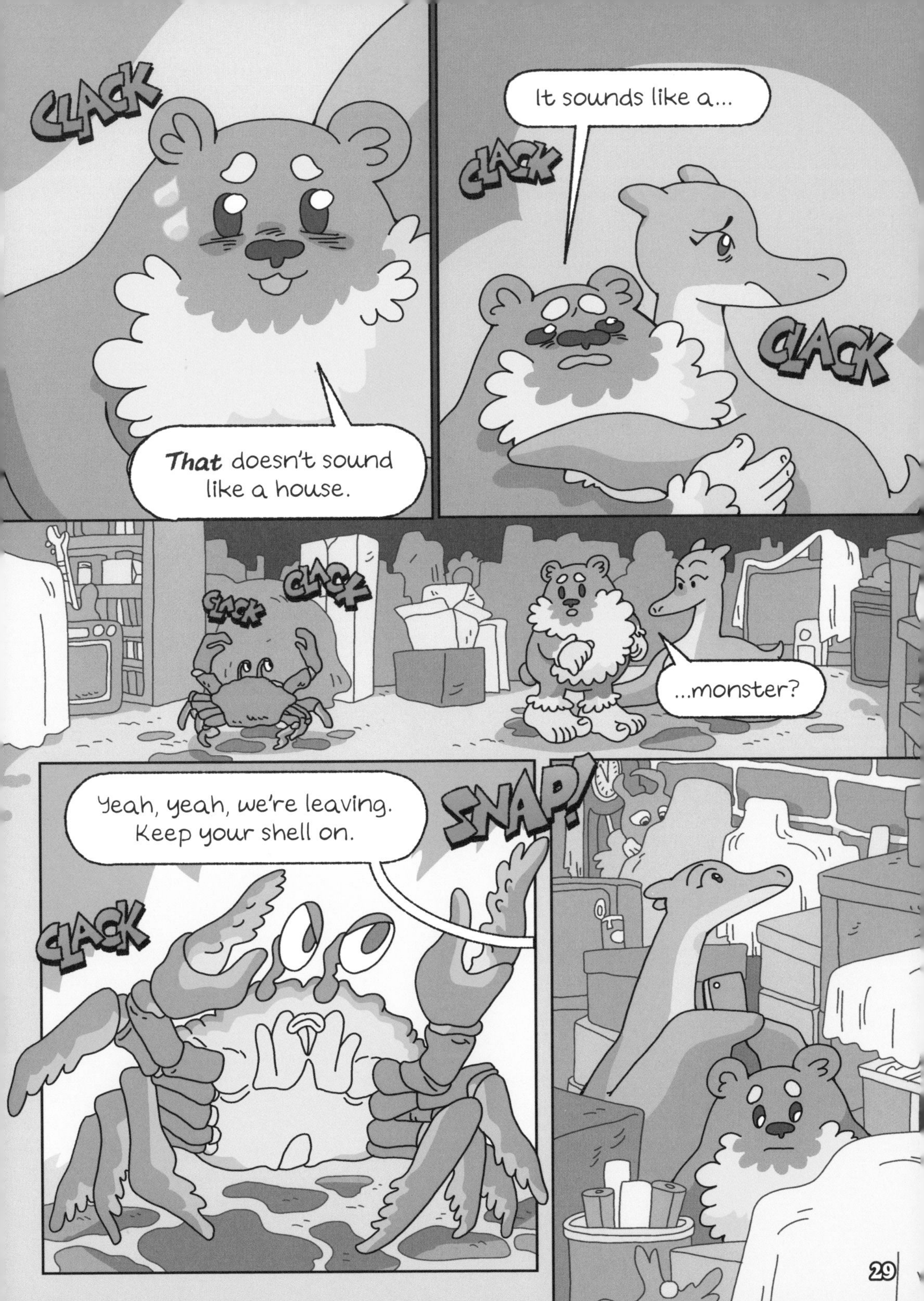
CLACK
That doesn't sound like a house.
It sounds like a...
CLACK
CLACK
CLACK
CLACK
...monster?
Yeah, yeah, we're leaving. Keep your shell on.
CLACK
SNAP!

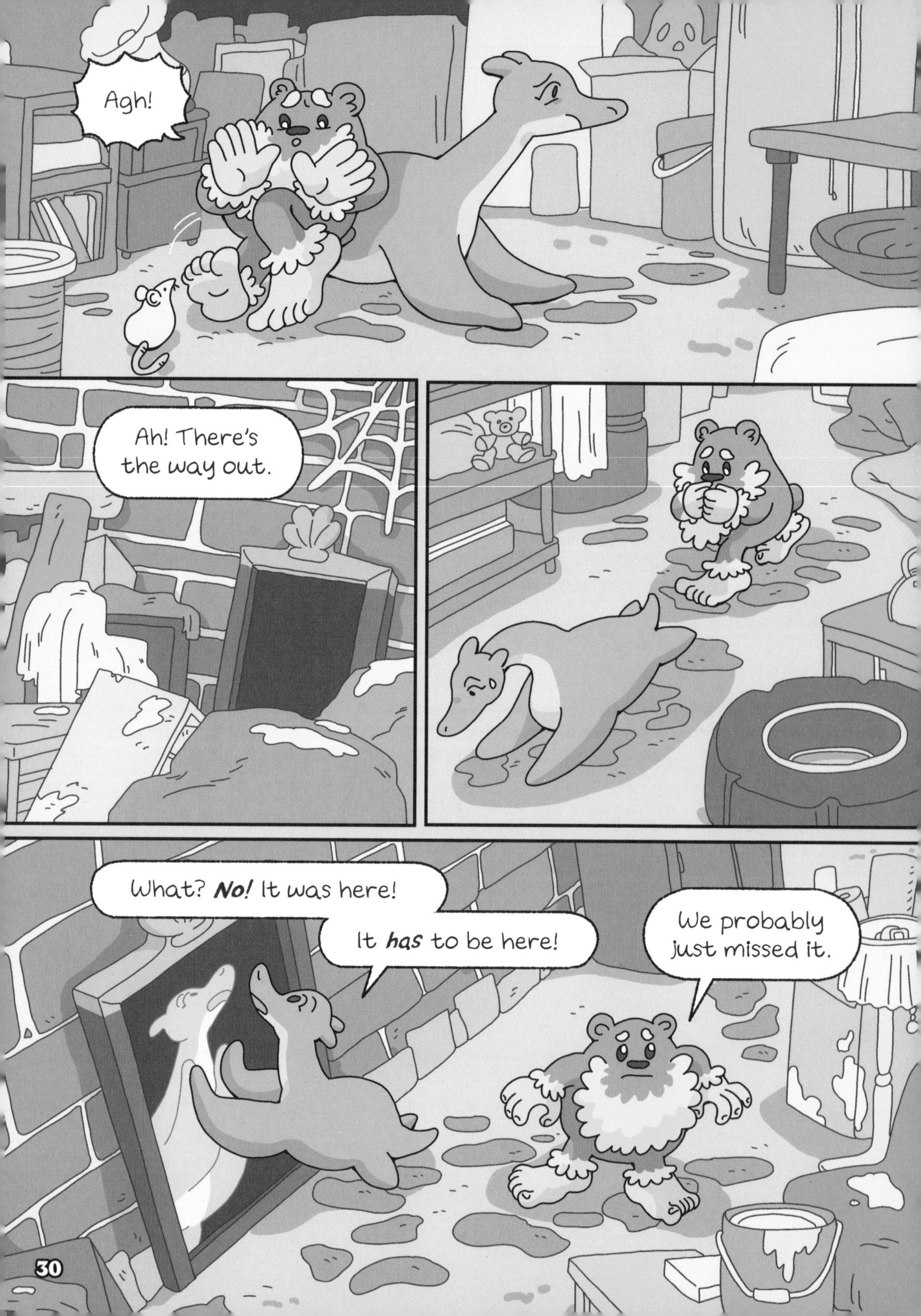
Agh!
Ah! There's the way out.
What? **No!** It was here!
It ***has*** to be here!
We probably just missed it.

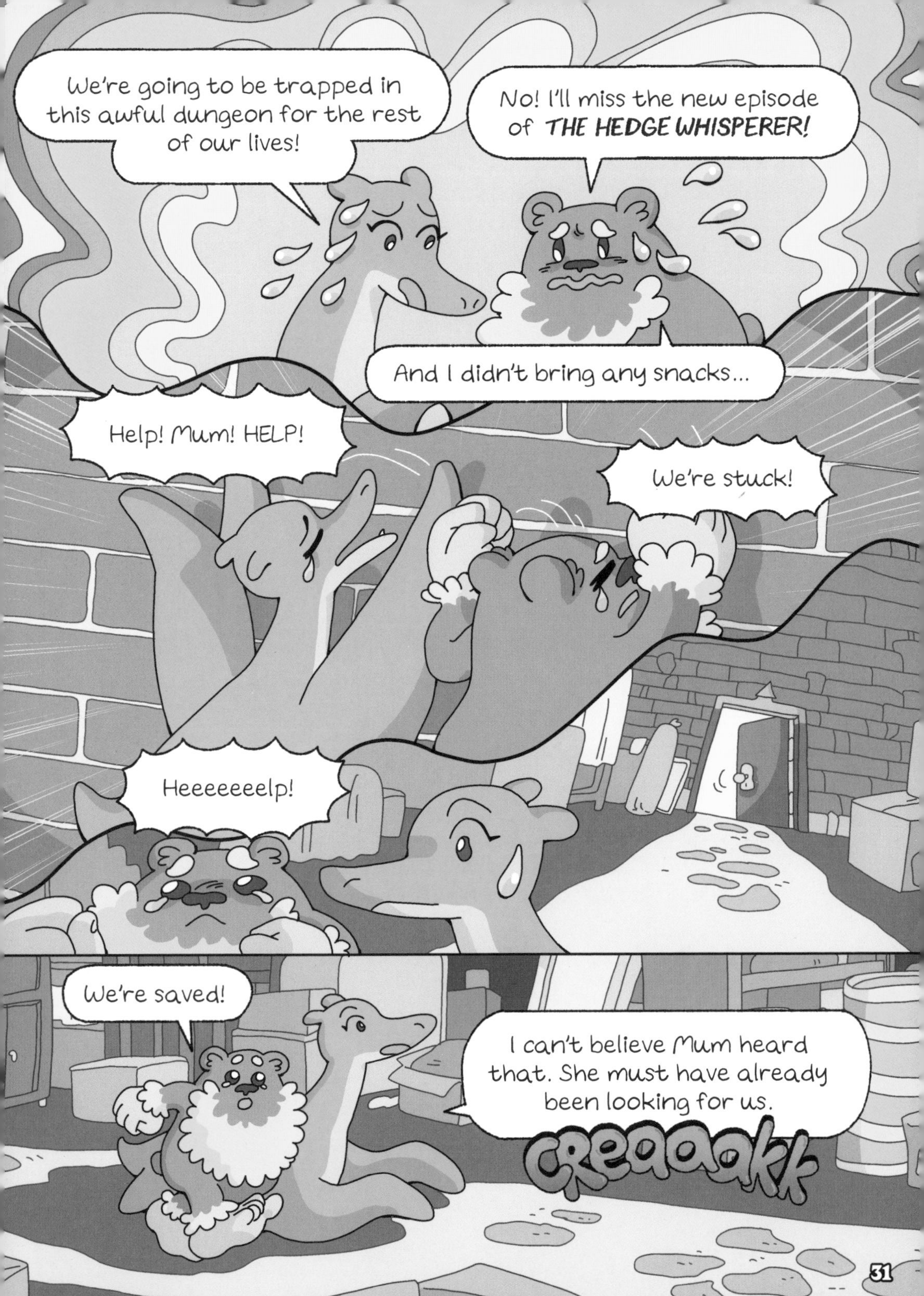
We're going to be trapped in this awful dungeon for the rest of our lives!
No! I'll miss the new episode of THE HEDGE WHISPERER!
And I didn't bring any snacks...
Help! Mum! HELP!
We're stuck!
Heeeeeeelp!
We're saved!
I can't believe Mum heard that. She must have already been looking for us.
CREAAAKK

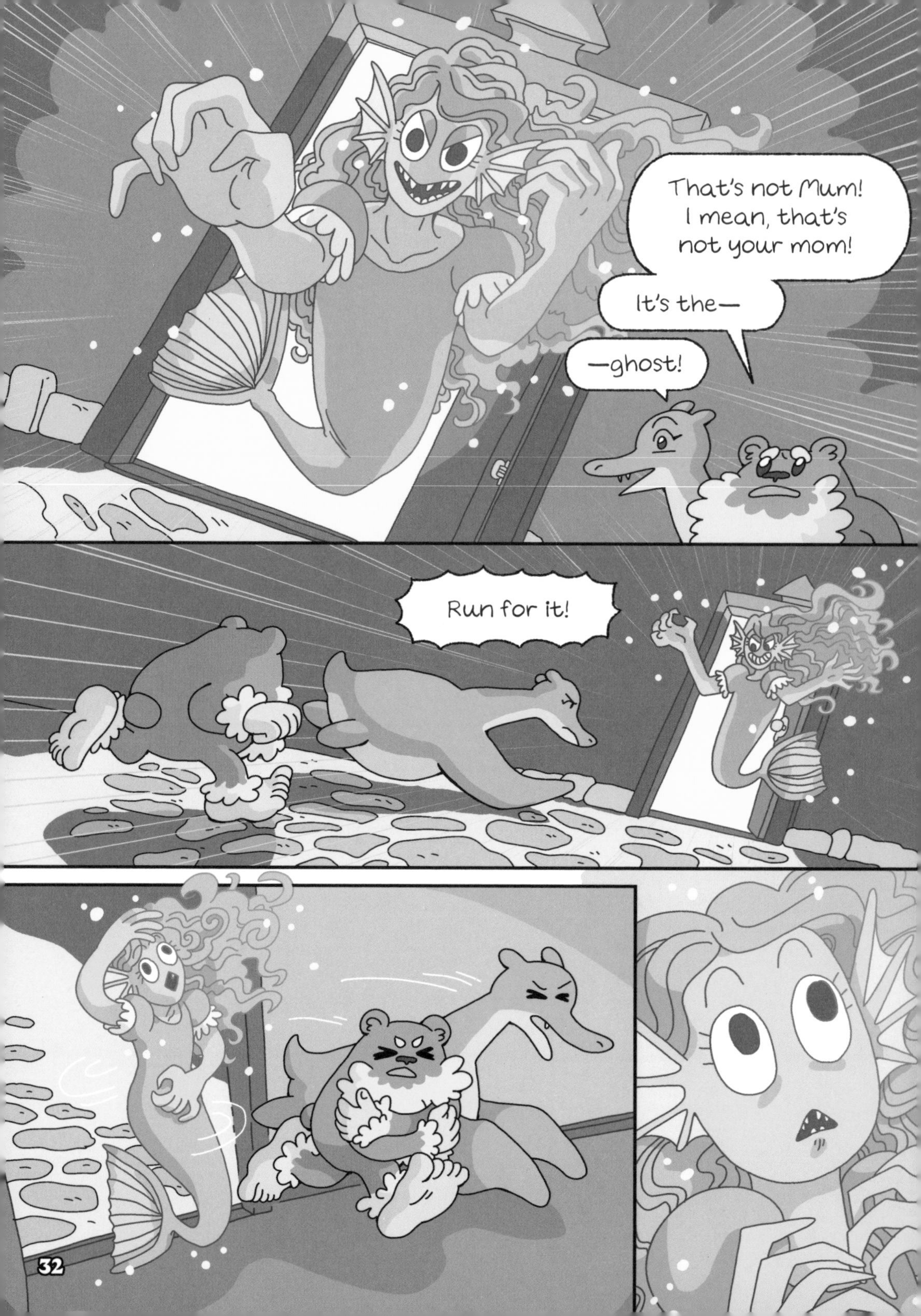
That's not Mum!
I mean, that's
not your mom!
It's the—
—ghost!
Run for it!

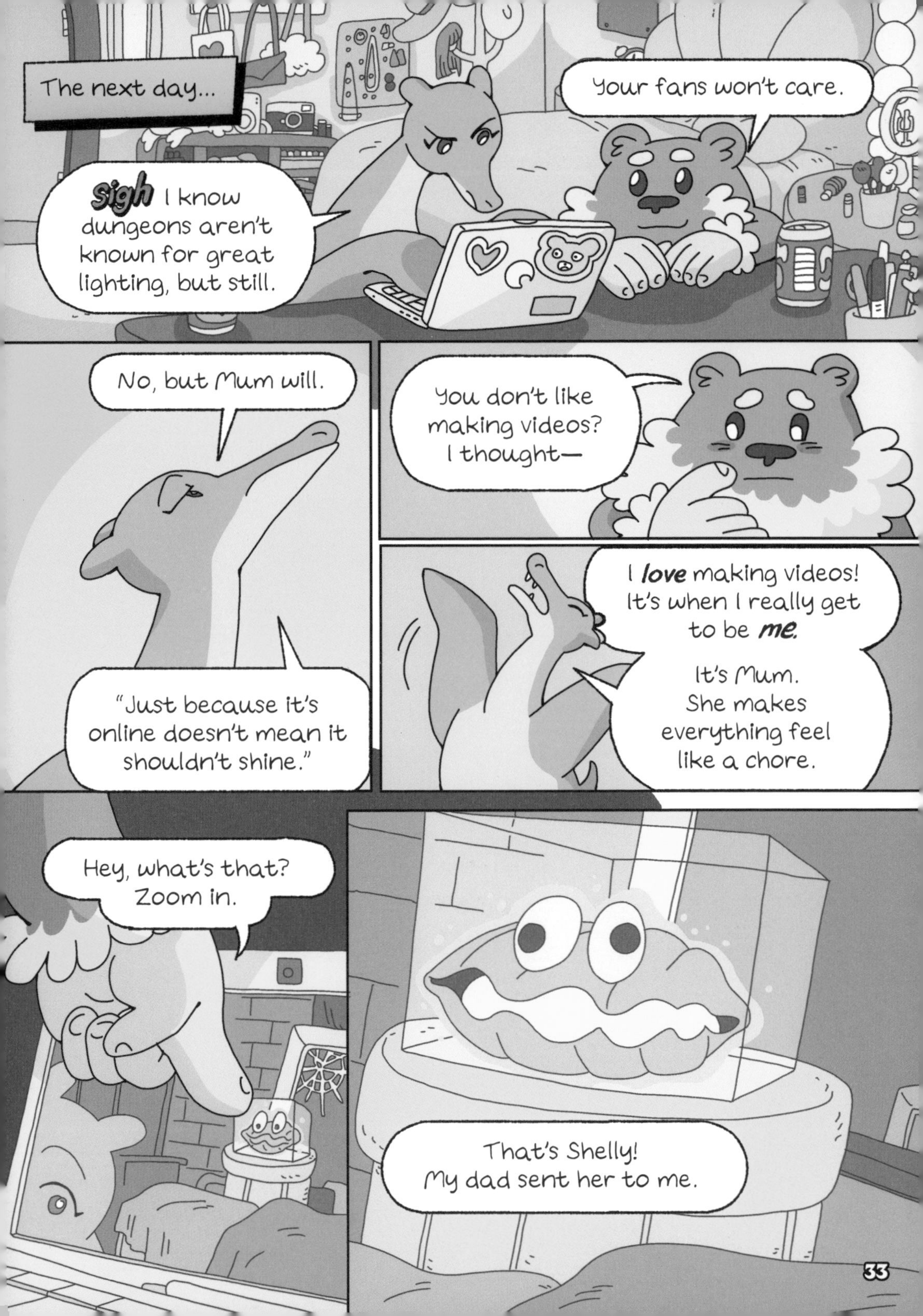
The next day...
Your fans won't care.
sigh I know dungeons aren't known for great lighting, but still.
No, but Mum will.
You don't like making videos? I thought—
"Just because it's online doesn't mean it shouldn't shine."
I *love* making videos! It's when I really get to be *me.*
It's Mum. She makes everything feel like a chore.
Hey, what's that? Zoom in.
That's Shelly! My dad sent her to me.

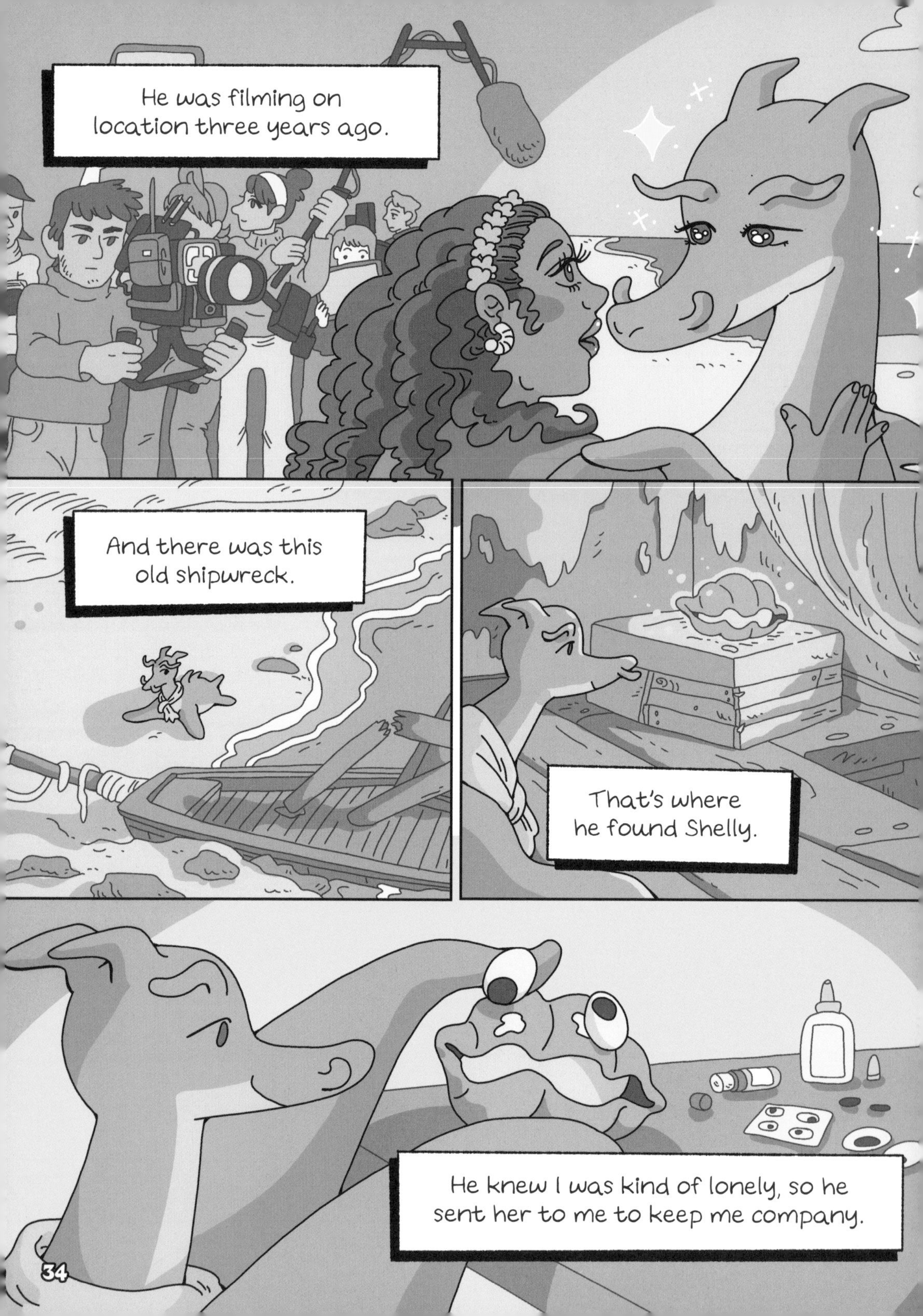
He was filming on location three years ago.
And there was this old shipwreck.
That's where he found Shelly.
He knew I was kind of lonely, so he sent her to me to keep me company.

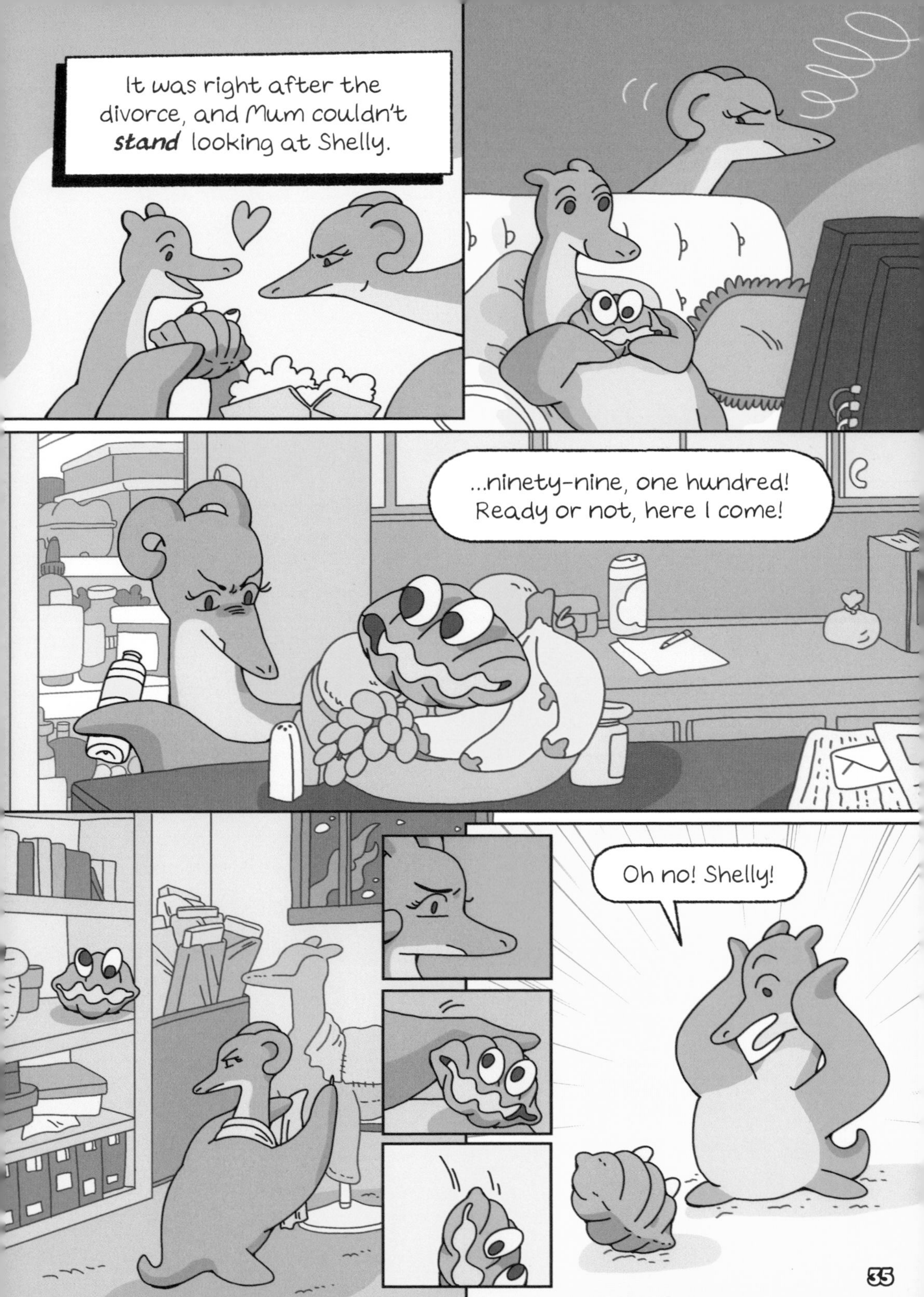
It was right after the divorce, and Mum couldn't **stand** looking at Shelly.
...ninety-nine, one hundred! Ready or not, here I come!
Oh no! Shelly!

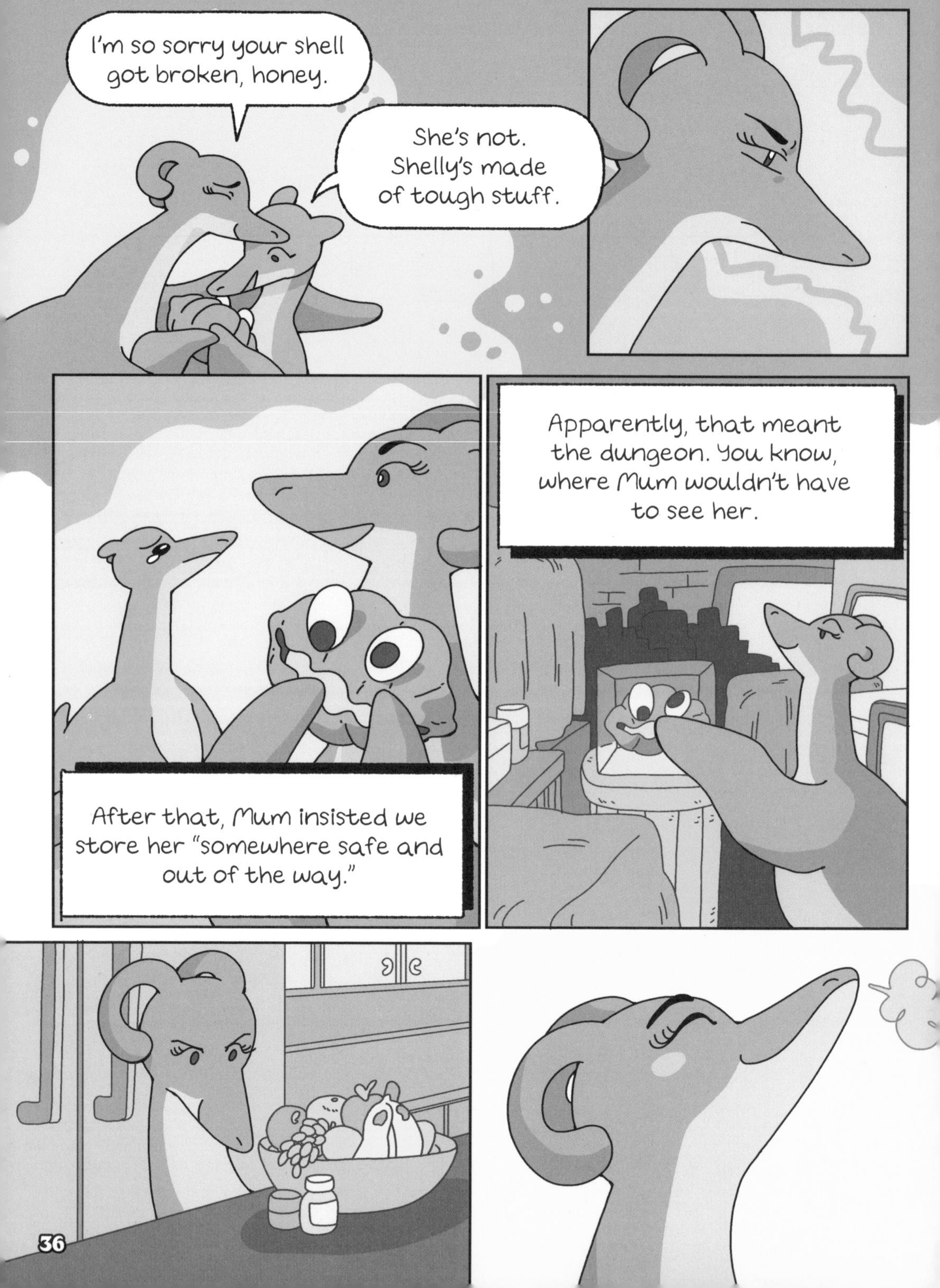

I'm so sorry your shell got broken, honey.
She's not. Shelly's made of tough stuff.
After that, Mum insisted we store her "somewhere safe and out of the way."
Apparently, that meant the dungeon. You know, where Mum wouldn't have to see her.

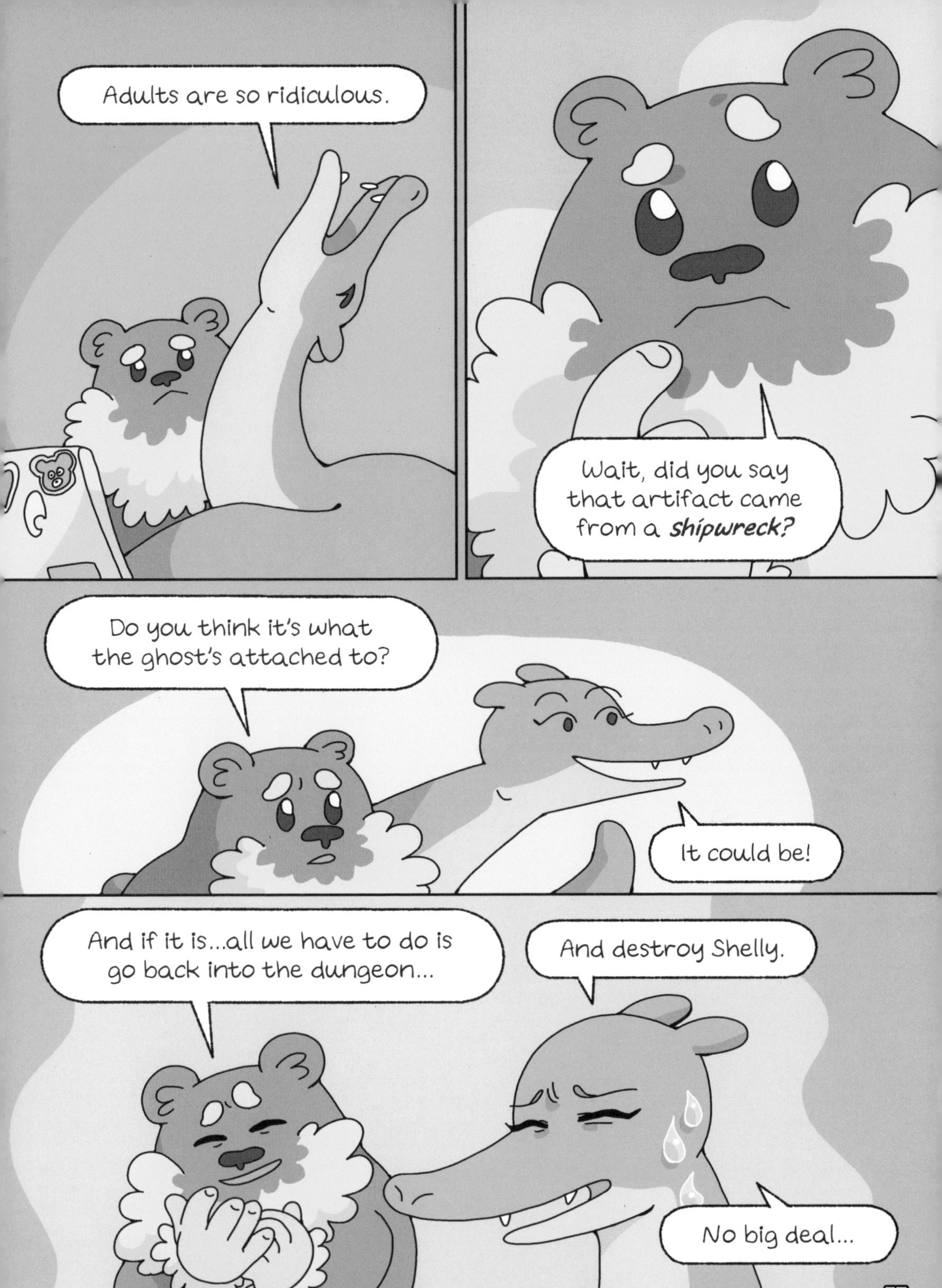
Adults are so ridiculous.
Wait, did you say that artifact came from a ***shipwreck?***
Do you think it's what the ghost's attached to?
It could be!
And if it is...all we have to do is go back into the dungeon...
And destroy Shelly.
No big deal...

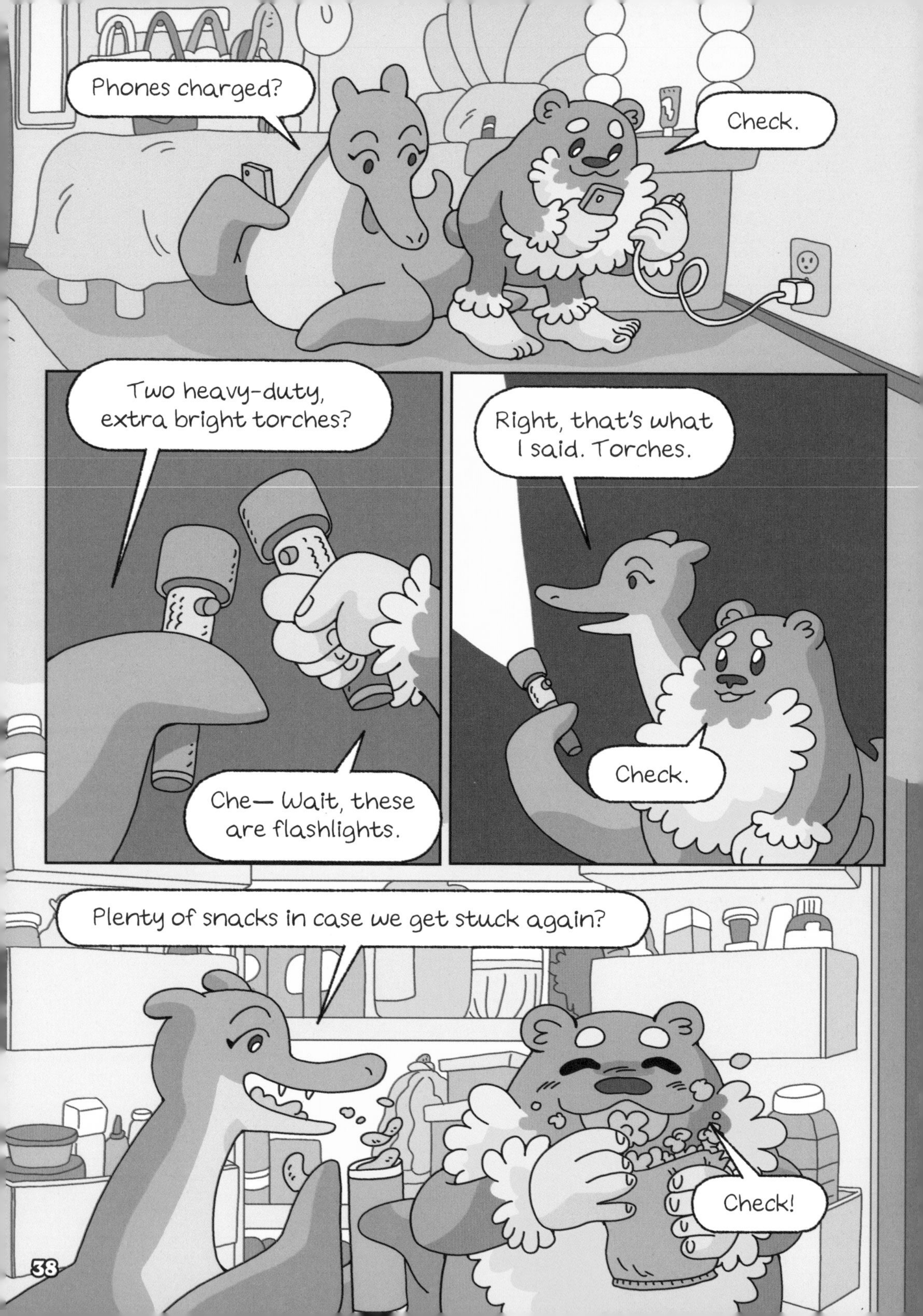
Phones charged?
Check.
Two heavy-duty, extra bright torches?
Che— Wait, these are flashlights.
Right, that's what I said. Torches.
Check.
Plenty of snacks in case we get stuck again?
Check!

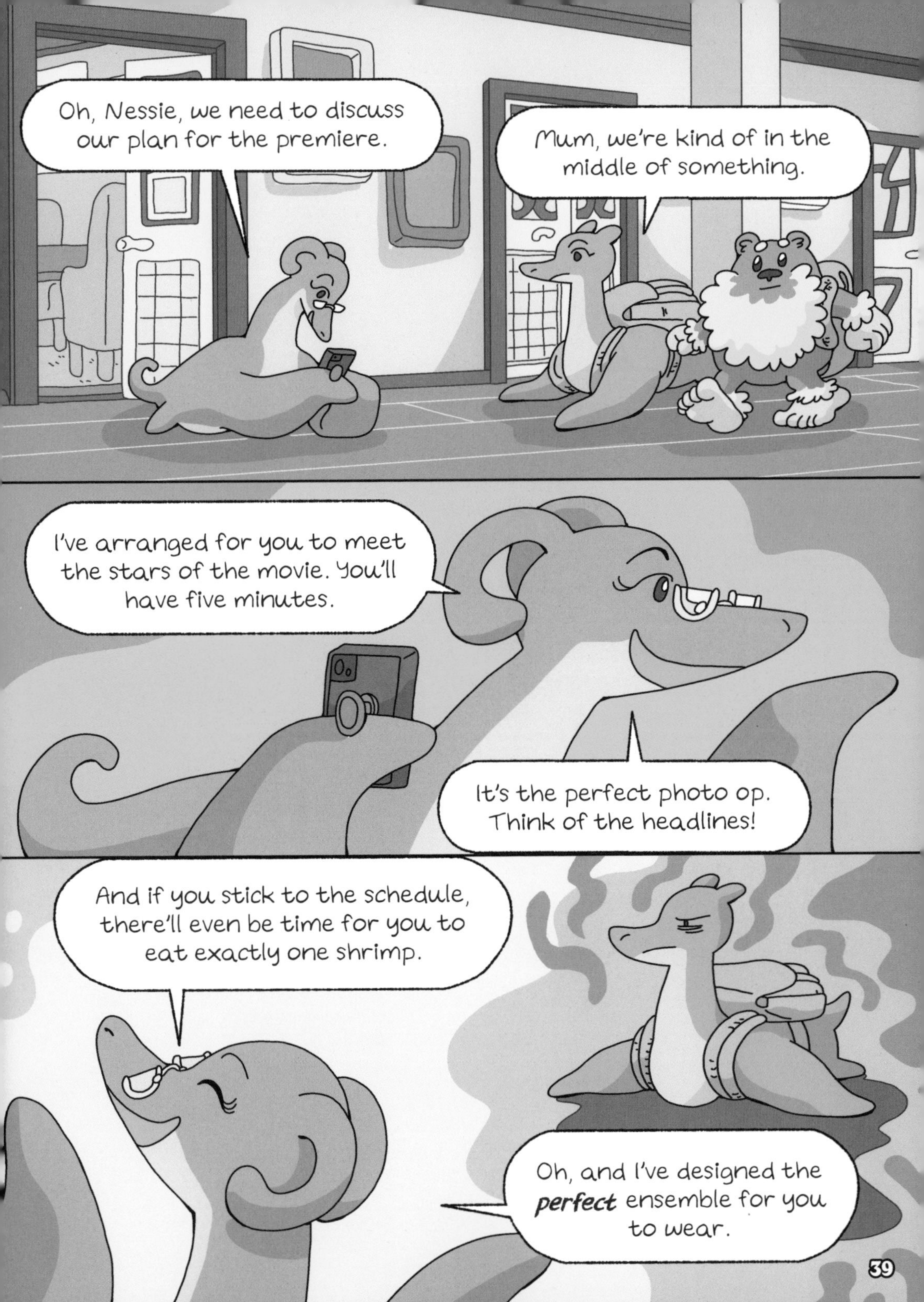

Oh, Nessie, we need to discuss our plan for the premiere.
Mum, we're kind of in the middle of something.
I've arranged for you to meet the stars of the movie. You'll have five minutes.
It's the perfect photo op. Think of the headlines!
And if you stick to the schedule, there'll even be time for you to eat exactly one shrimp.
Oh, and I've designed the *perfect* ensemble for you to wear.

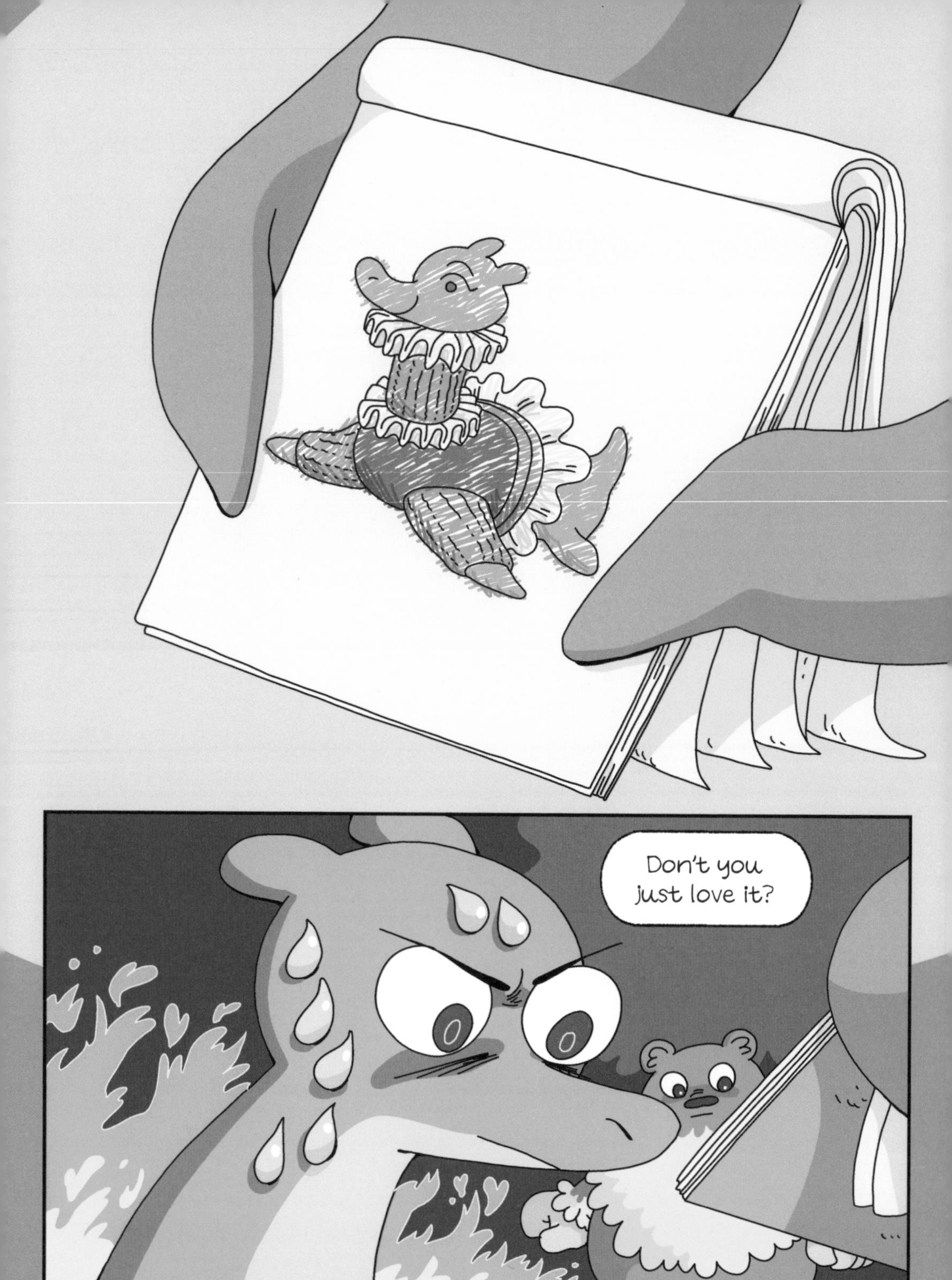
Don't you just love it?

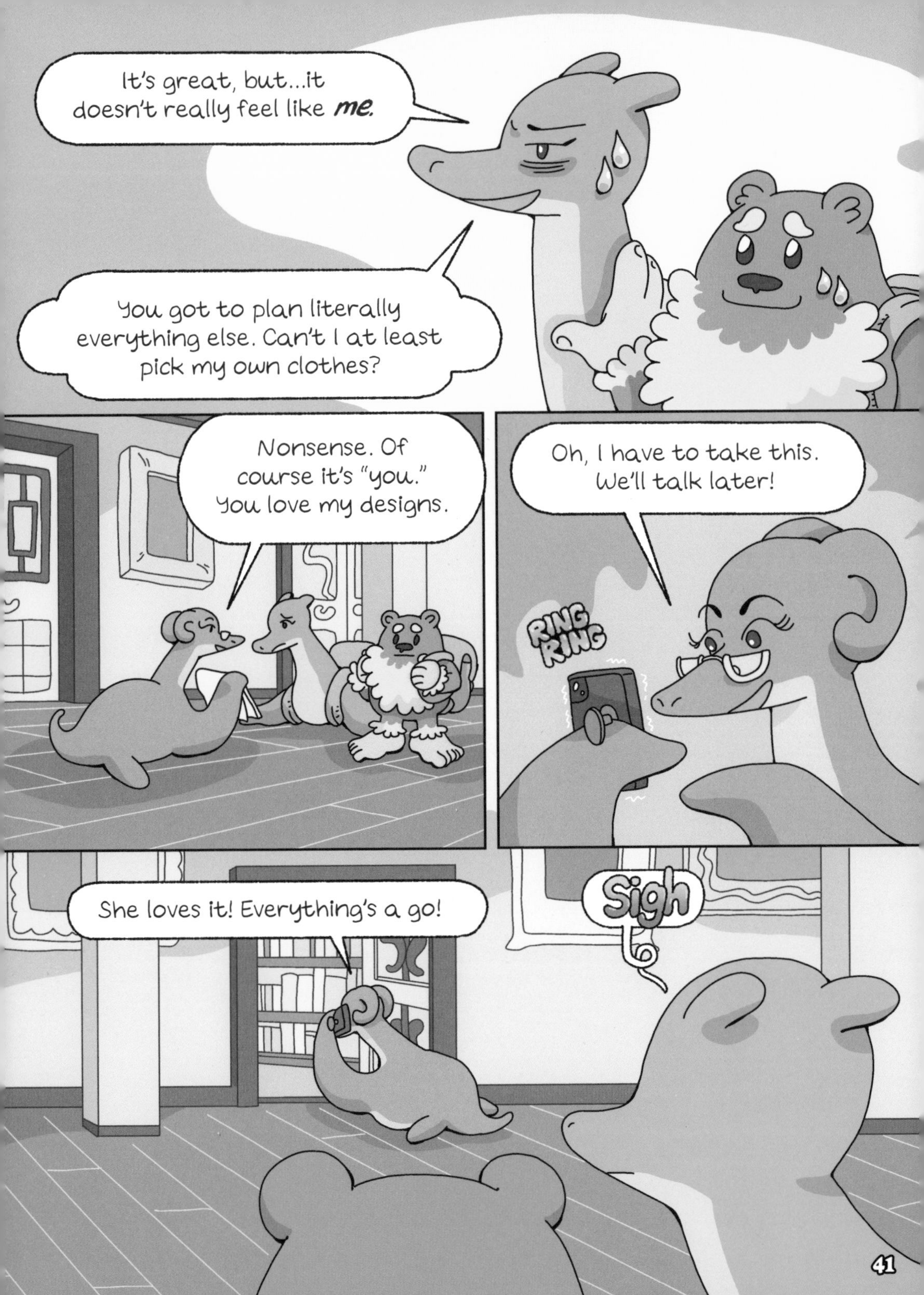
It's great, but...it doesn't really feel like *me.*
You got to plan literally everything else. Can't I at least pick my own clothes?
Nonsense. Of course it's "you." You love my designs.
Oh, I have to take this. We'll talk later!
RING RING
She loves it! Everything's a go!
Sigh

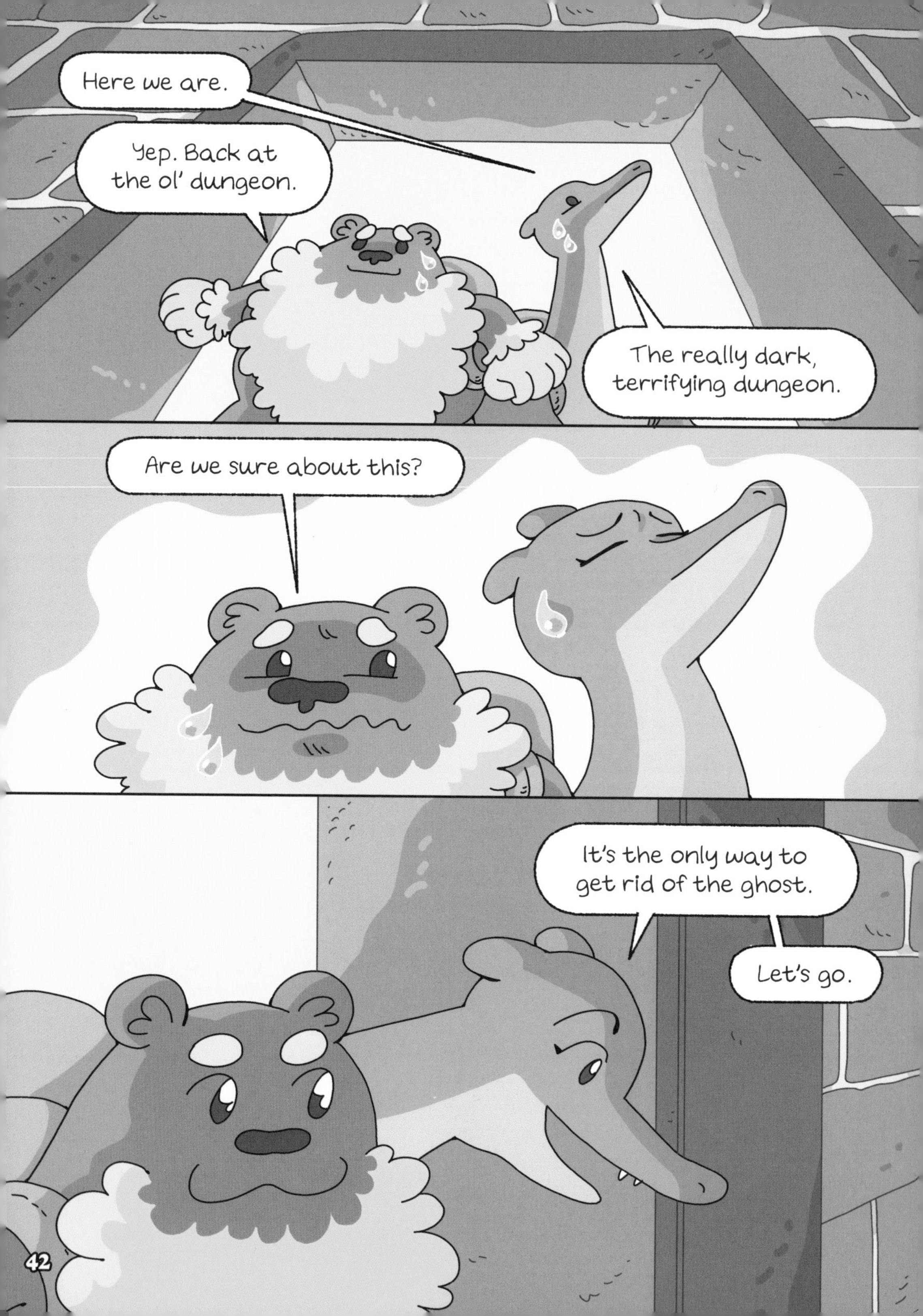
Here we are.
Yep. Back at the ol' dungeon.
The really dark, terrifying dungeon.
Are we sure about this?
It's the only way to get rid of the ghost.
Let's go.

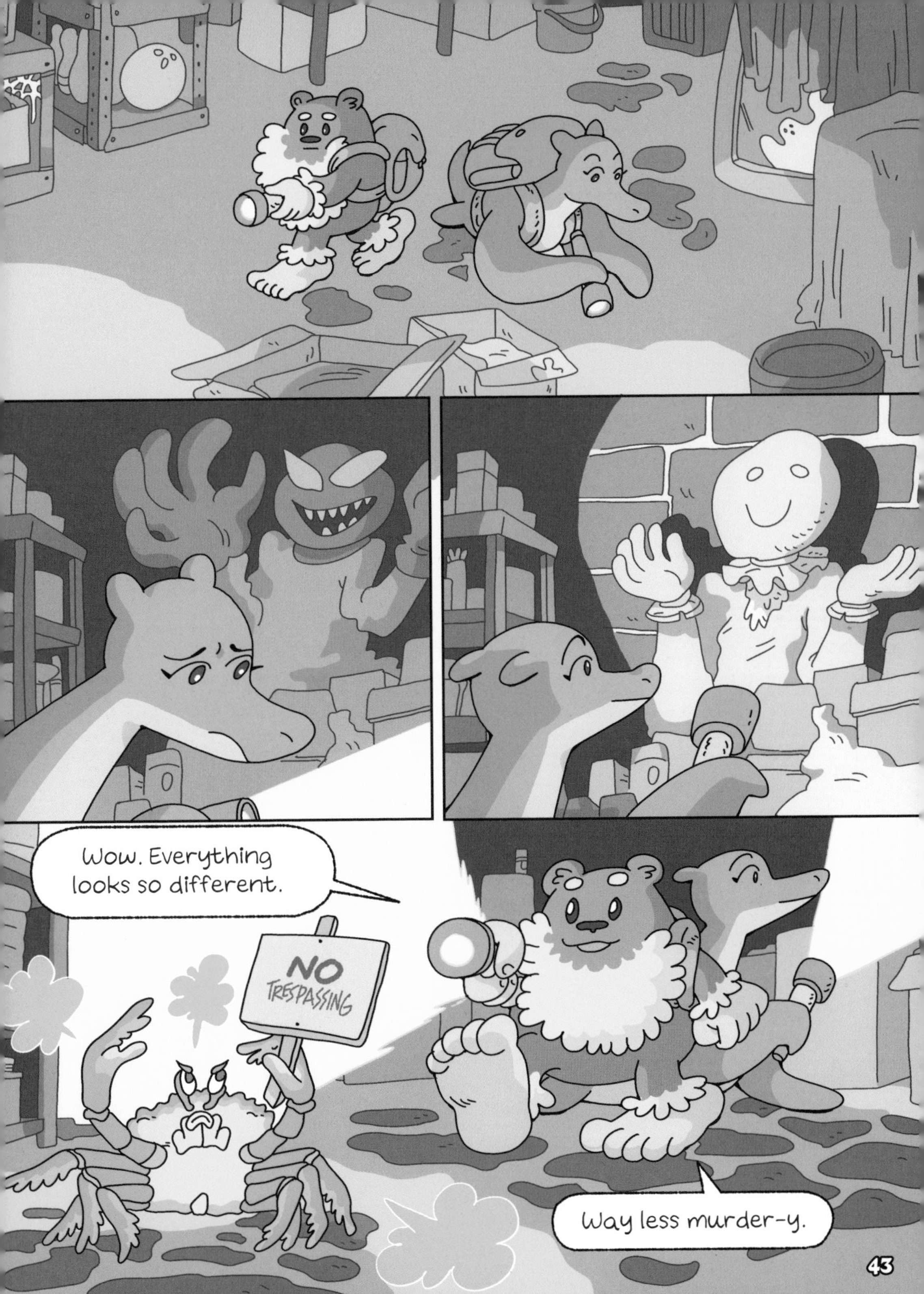
Wow. Everything looks so different.
NO TRESPASSING
Way less murder-y.

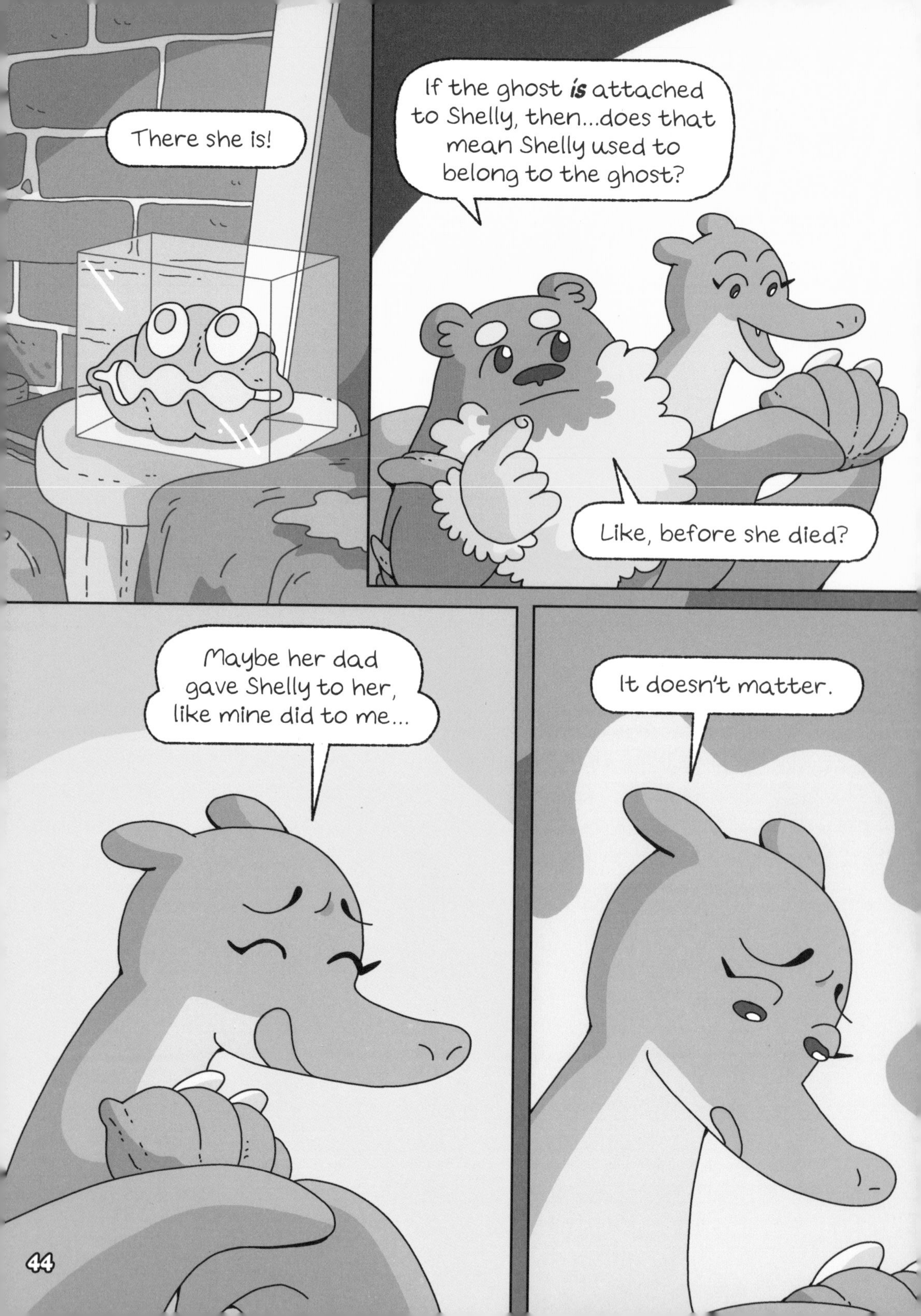
There she is!
If the ghost **is** attached to Shelly, then...does that mean Shelly used to belong to the ghost?
Like, before she died?
Maybe her dad gave Shelly to her, like mine did to me...
It doesn't matter.

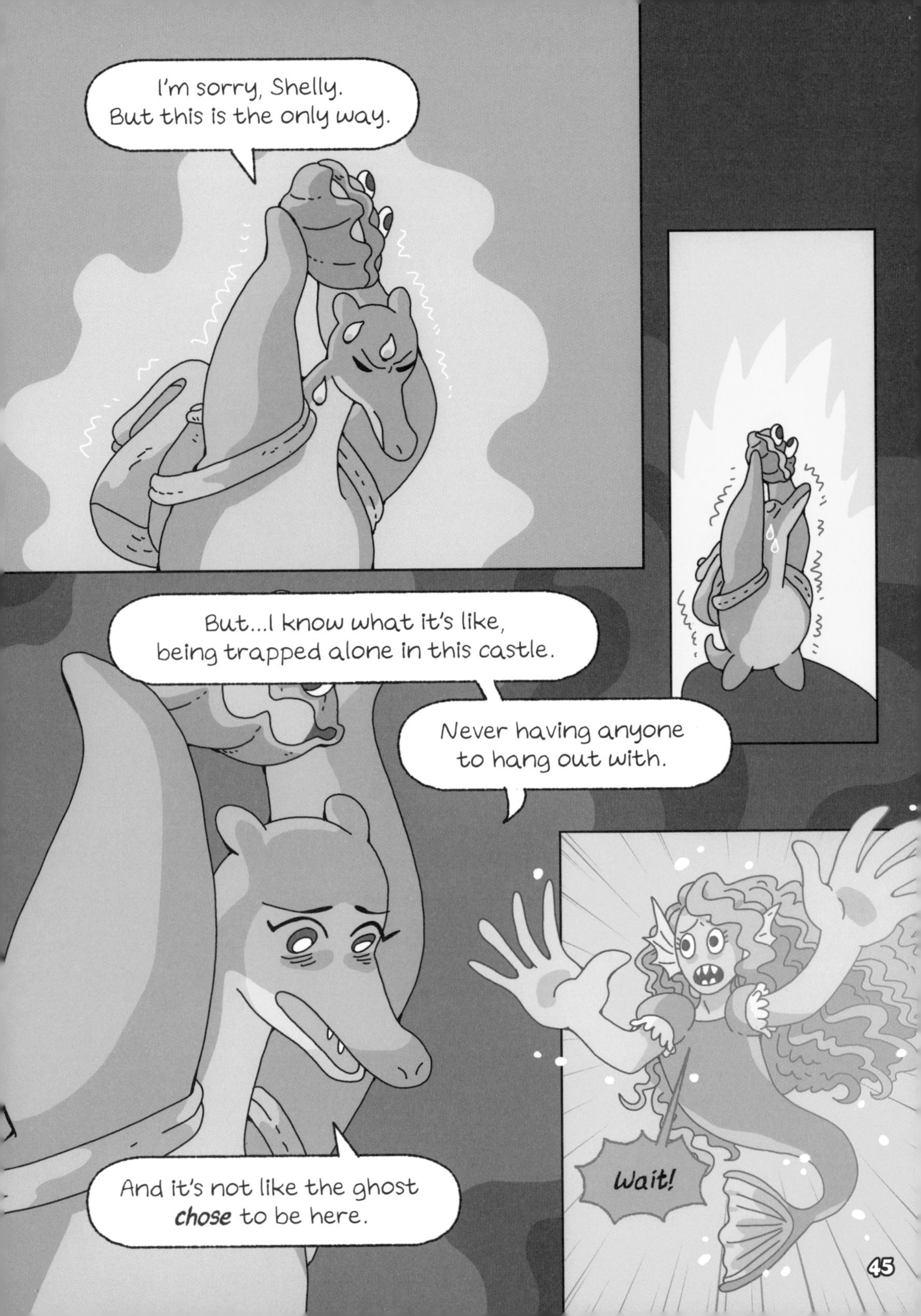
I'm sorry, Shelly.
But this is the only way.
But...I know what it's like, being trapped alone in this castle.
Never having anyone to hang out with.
And it's not like the ghost *chose* to be here.
Wait!

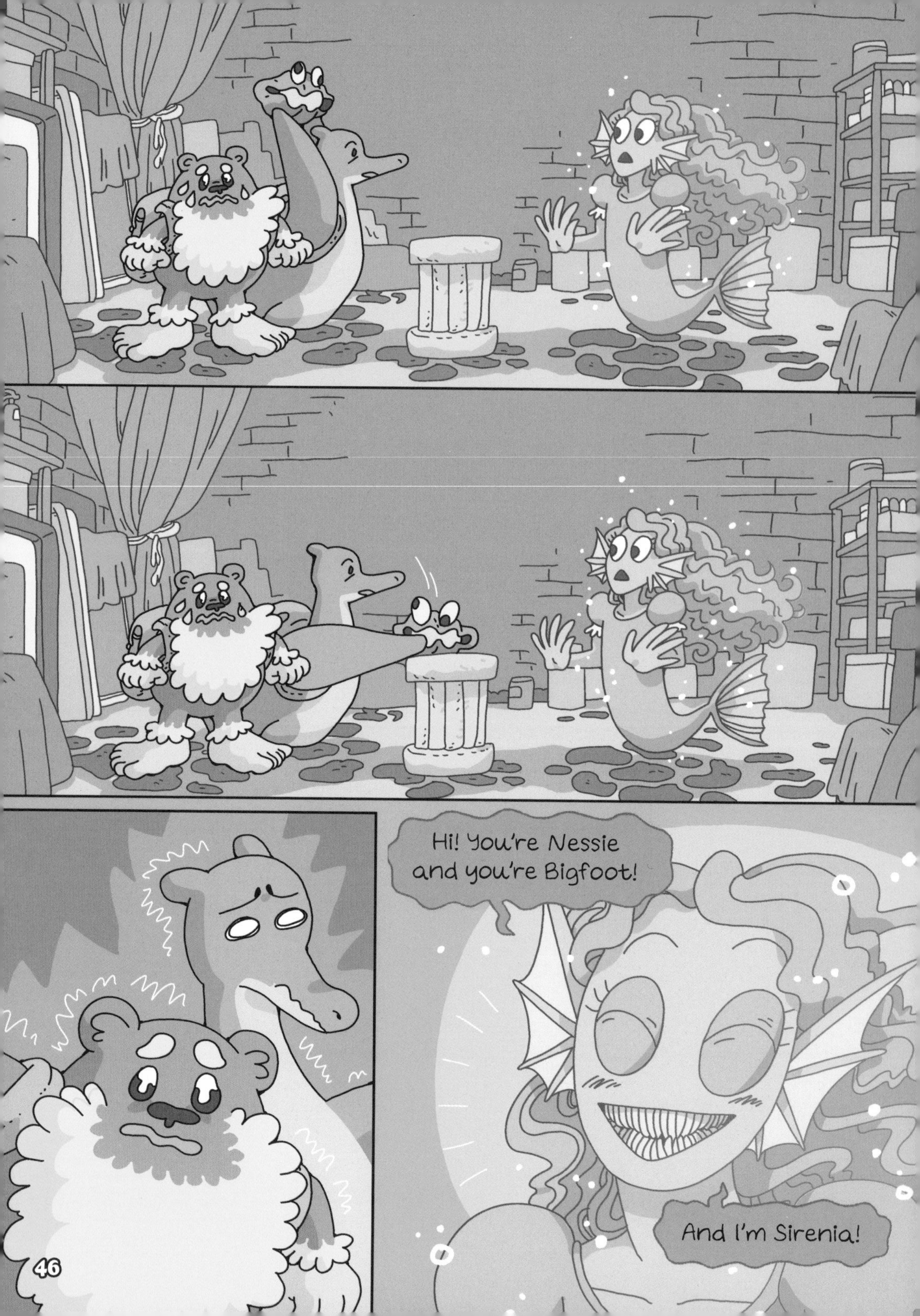
Hi! You're Nessie and you're Bigfoot!
And I'm Sirenia!

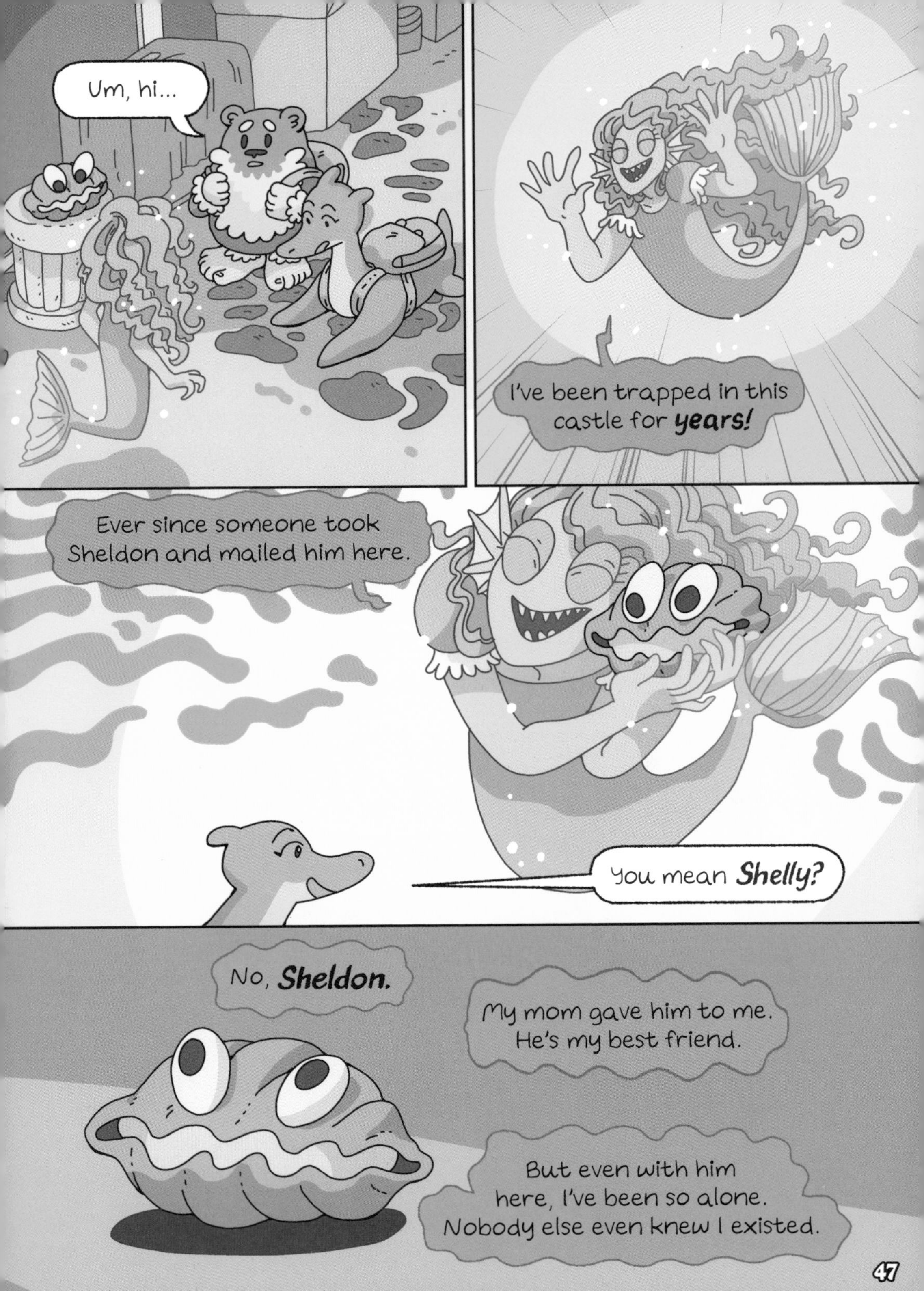
Um, hi...
I've been trapped in this castle for **years!**
Ever since someone took Sheldon and mailed him here.
You mean **Shelly?**
No, **Sheldon.**
My mom gave him to me. He's my best friend.
But even with him here, I've been so alone. Nobody else even knew I existed.

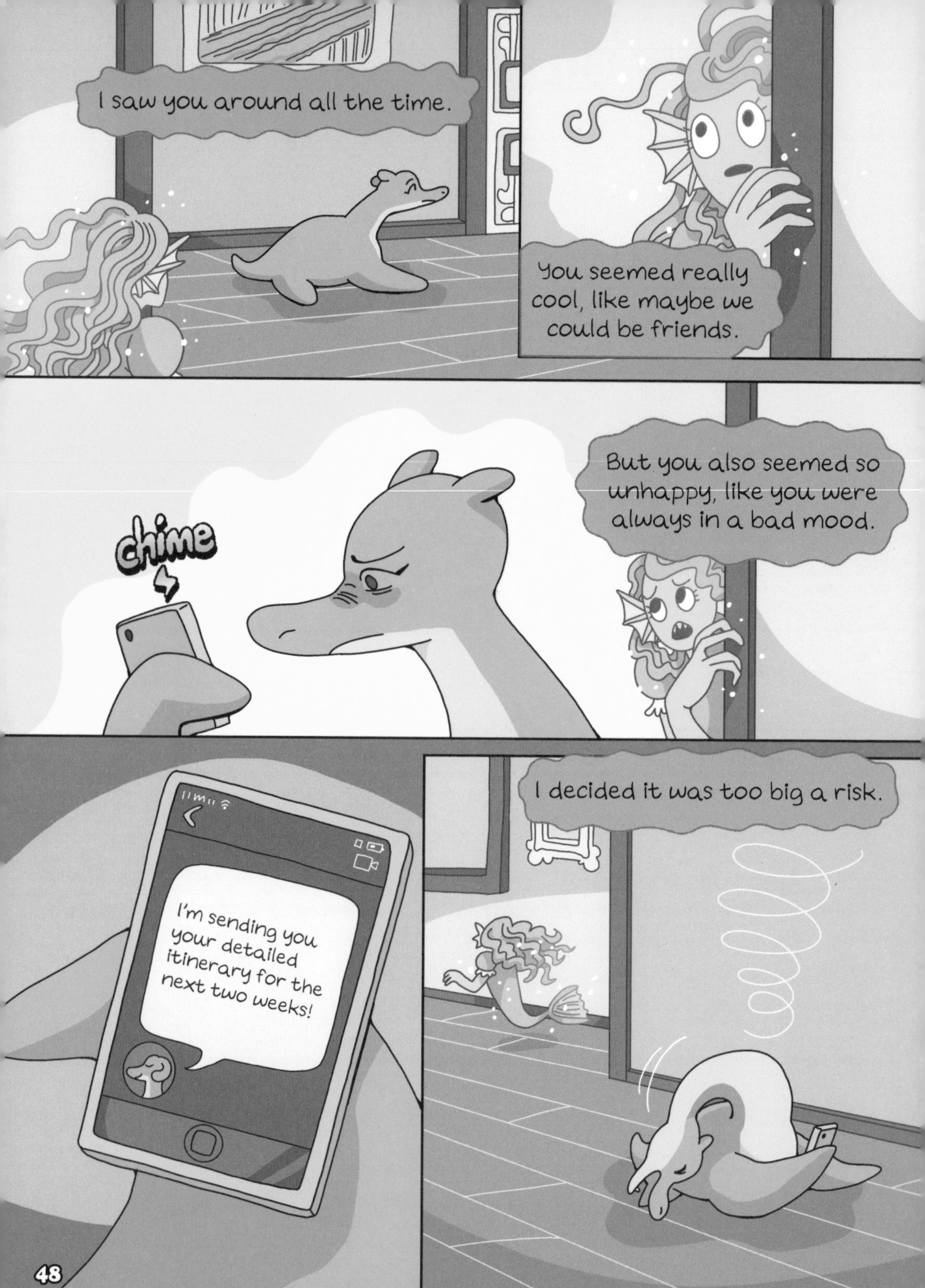
I saw you around all the time.
You seemed really cool, like maybe we could be friends.
But you also seemed so unhappy, like you were always in a bad mood.
chime
I'm sending you your detailed itinerary for the next two weeks!
I decided it was too big a risk.

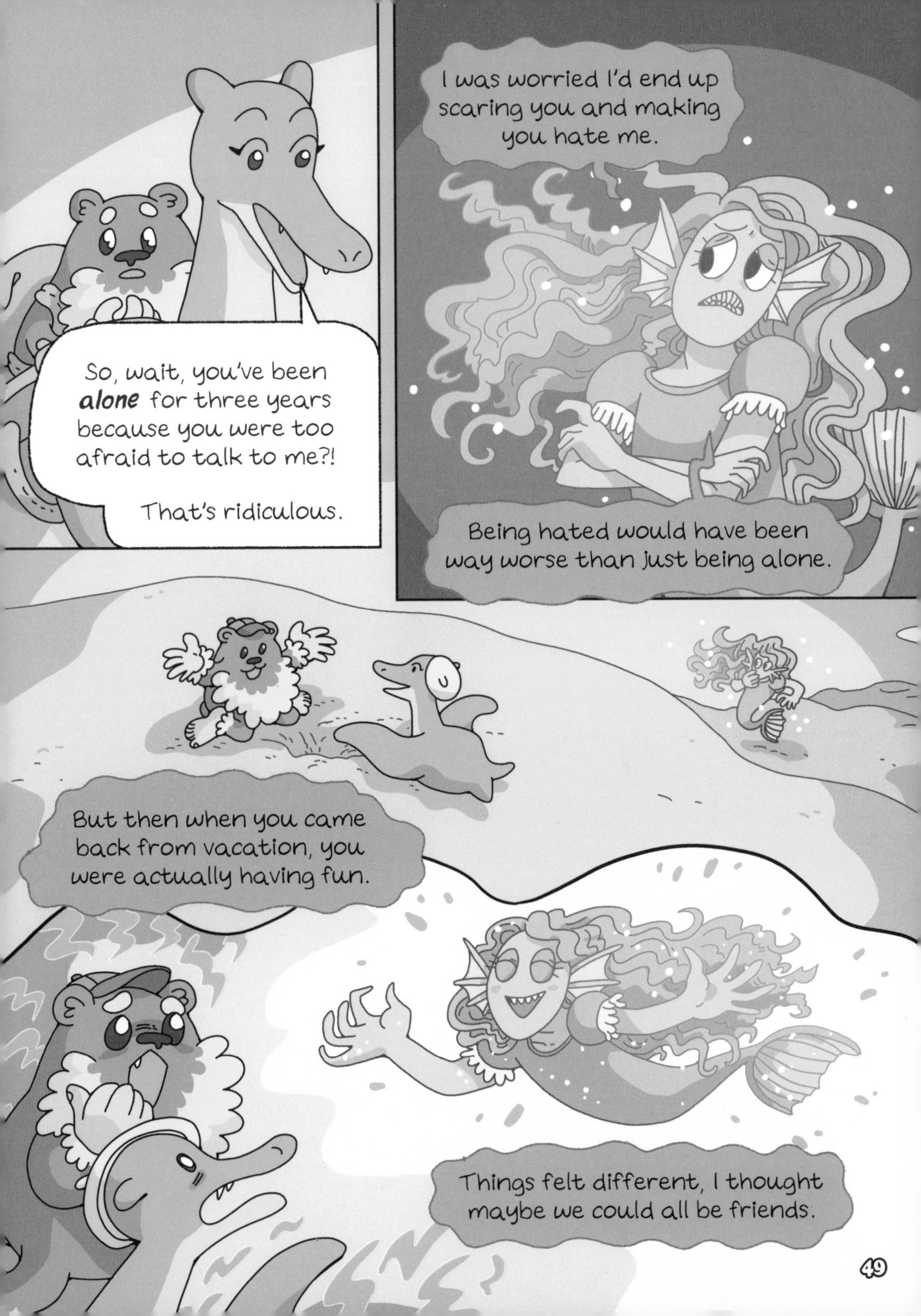
So, wait, you've been **alone** for three years because you were too afraid to talk to me?!
That's ridiculous.
I was worried I'd end up scaring you and making you hate me.
Being hated would have been way worse than just being alone.
But then when you came back from vacation, you were actually having fun.
Things felt different, I thought maybe we could all be friends.

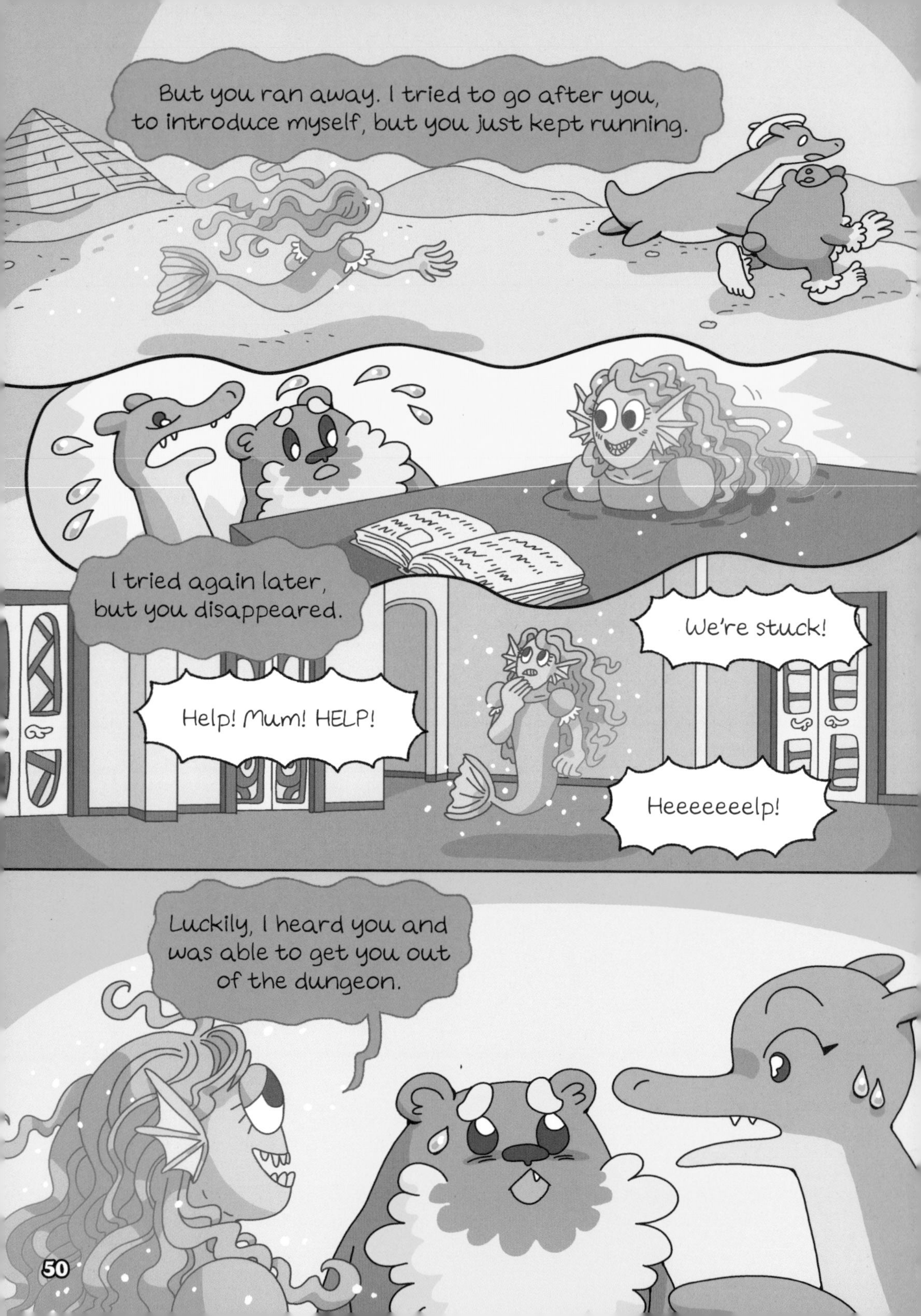
But you ran away. I tried to go after you, to introduce myself, but you just kept running.
I tried again later, but you disappeared.
Help! Mum! HELP!
We're stuck!
Heeeeeeelp!
Luckily, I heard you and was able to get you out of the dungeon.

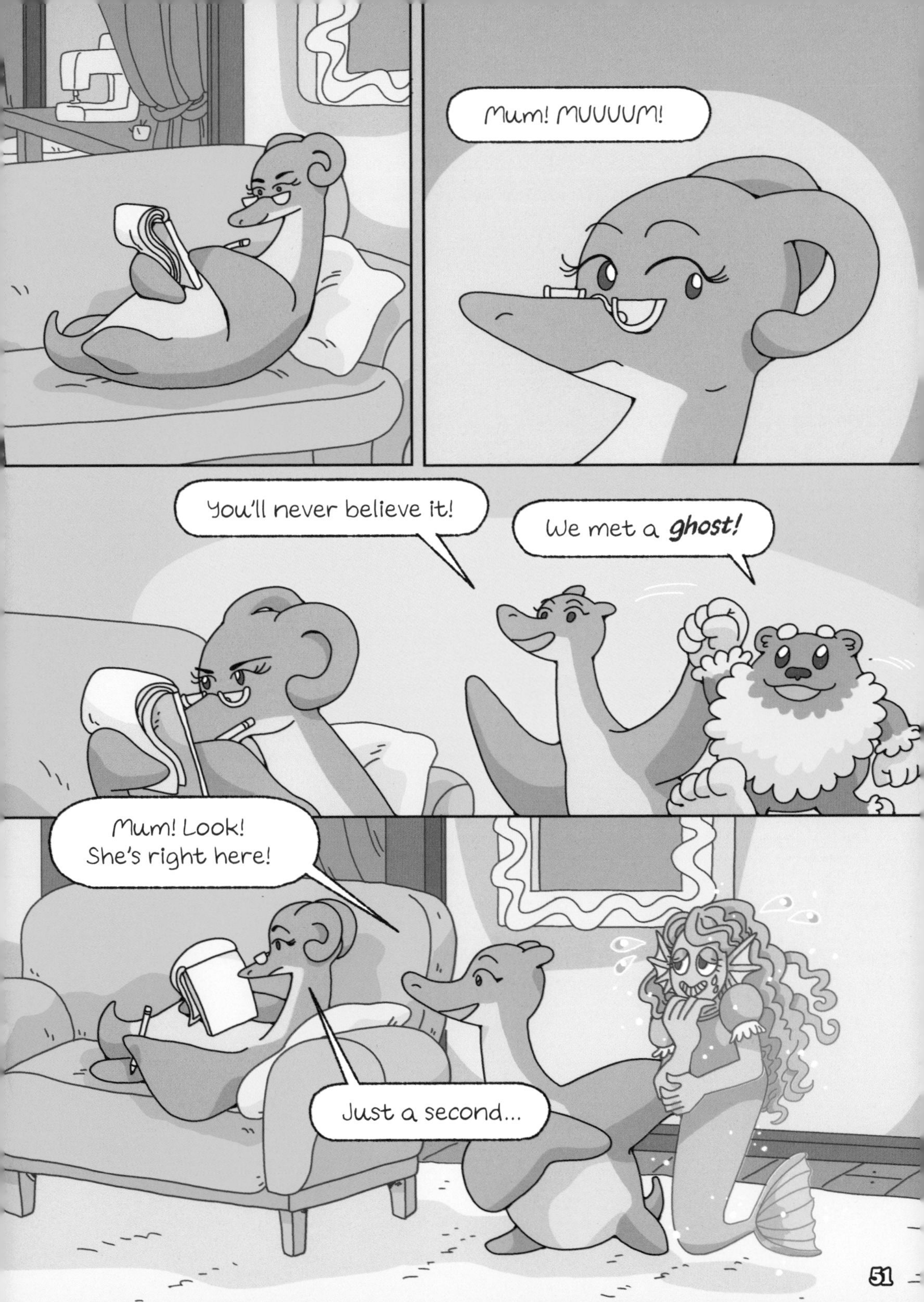
Mum! MUUUUM!
You'll never believe it!
We met a ***ghost!***
Mum! Look!
She's right here!
Just a second...

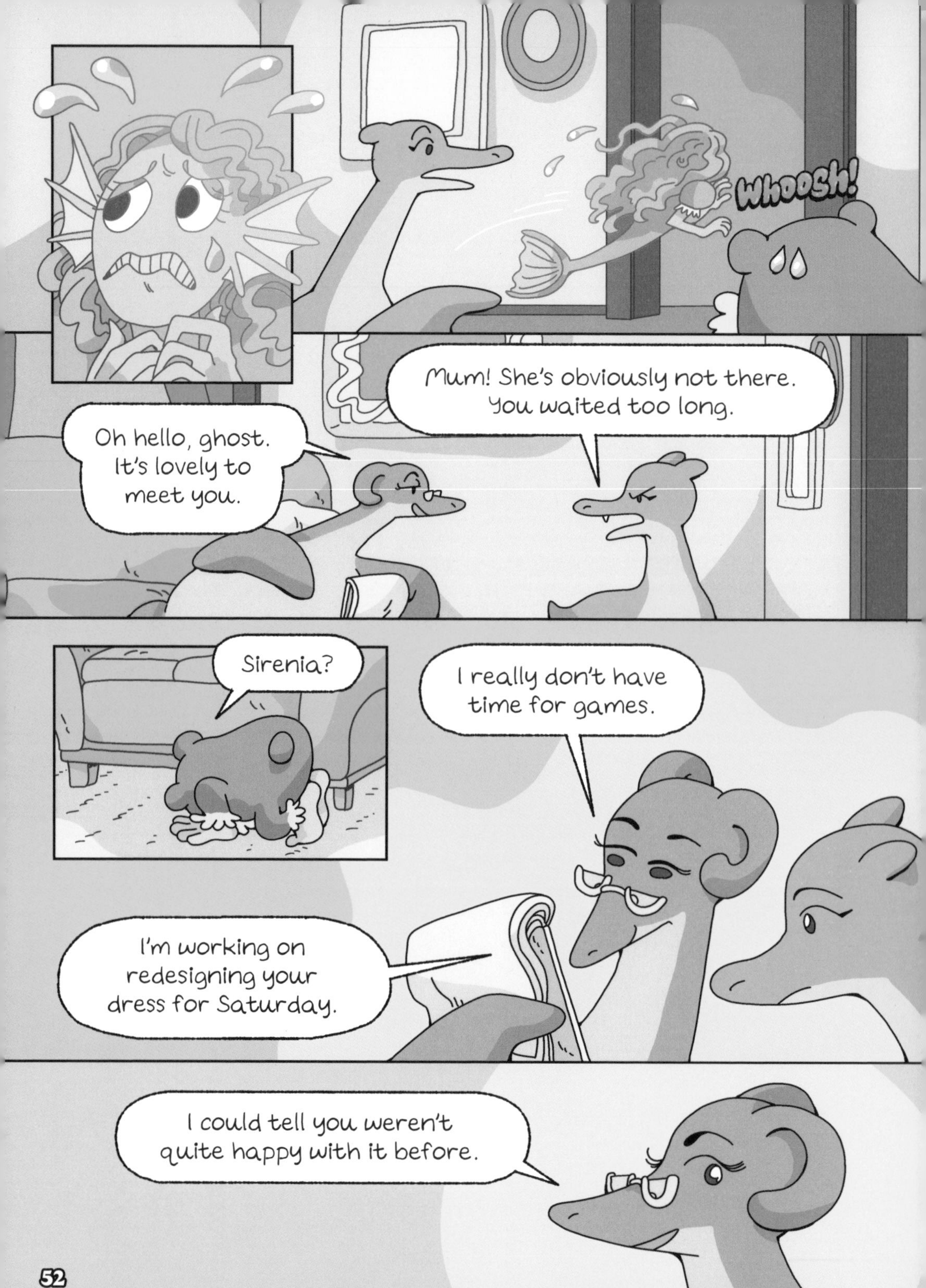
WHOOSH!
Oh hello, ghost. It's lovely to meet you.
Mum! She's obviously not there. You waited too long.
Sirenia?
I really don't have time for games.
I'm working on redesigning your dress for Saturday.
I could tell you weren't quite happy with it before.

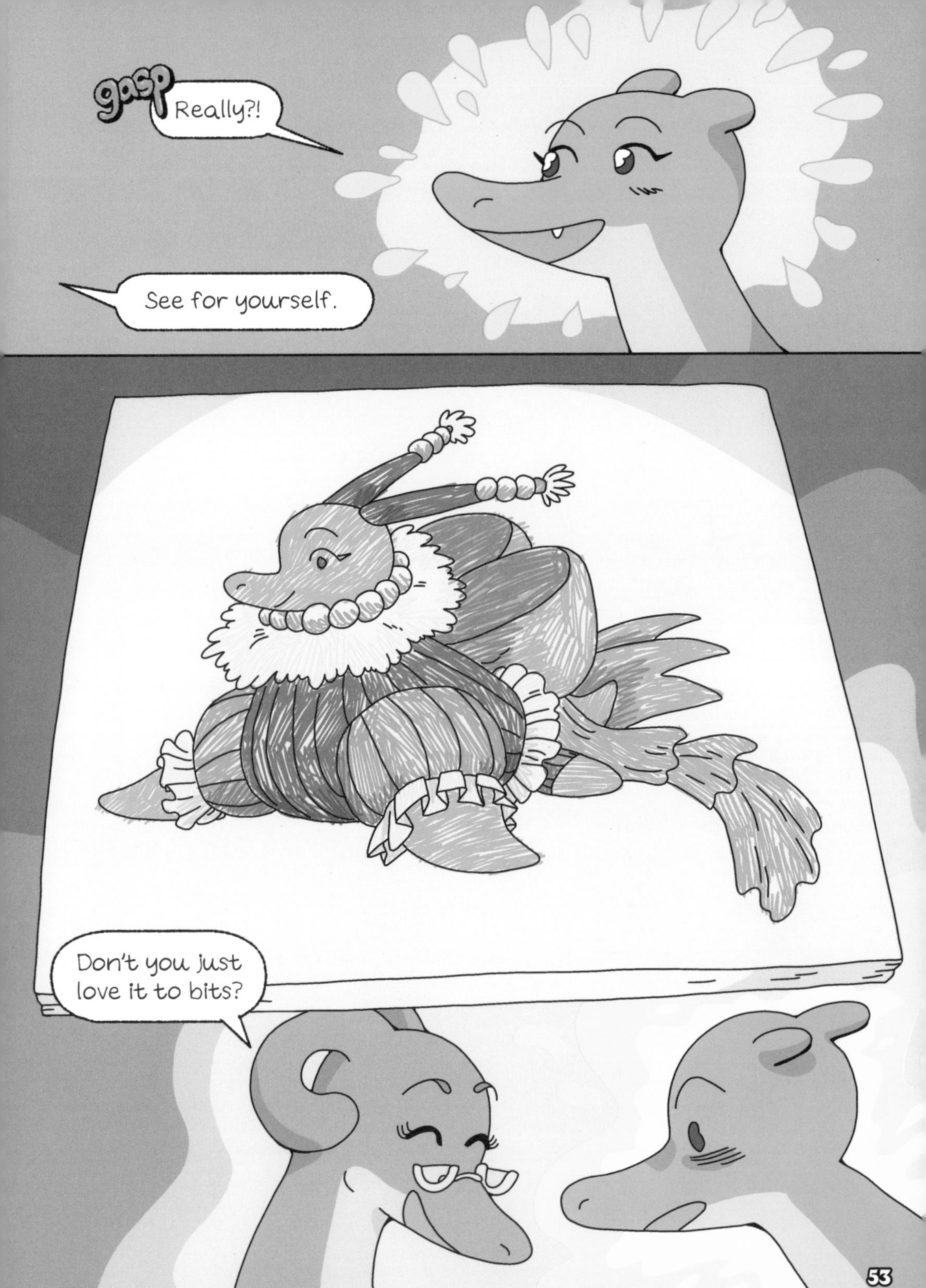
gasp
Really?!
See for yourself.
Don't you just love it to bits?

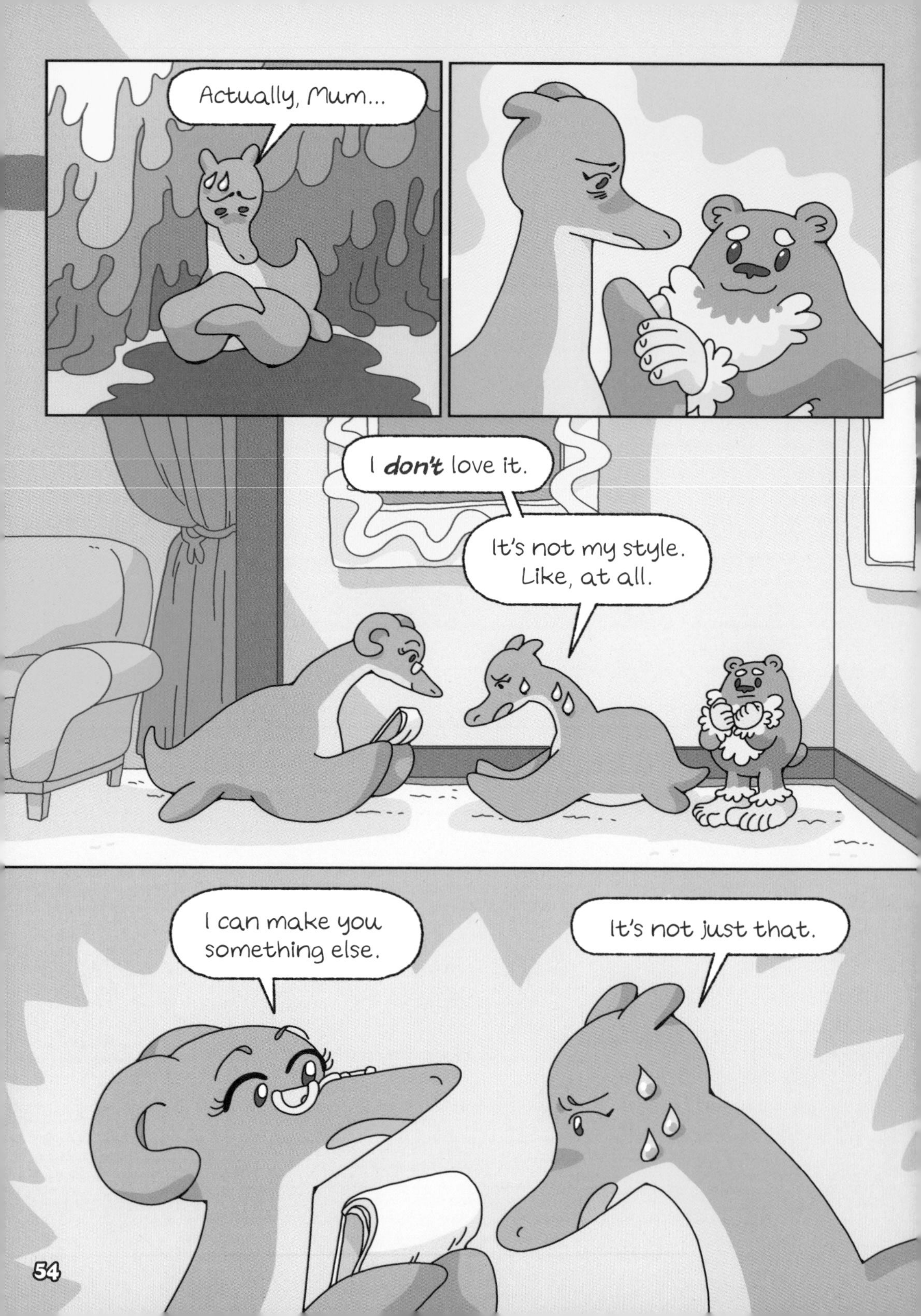
Actually, Mum...
I **don't** love it.
It's not my style. Like, at all.
I can make you something else.
It's not just that.

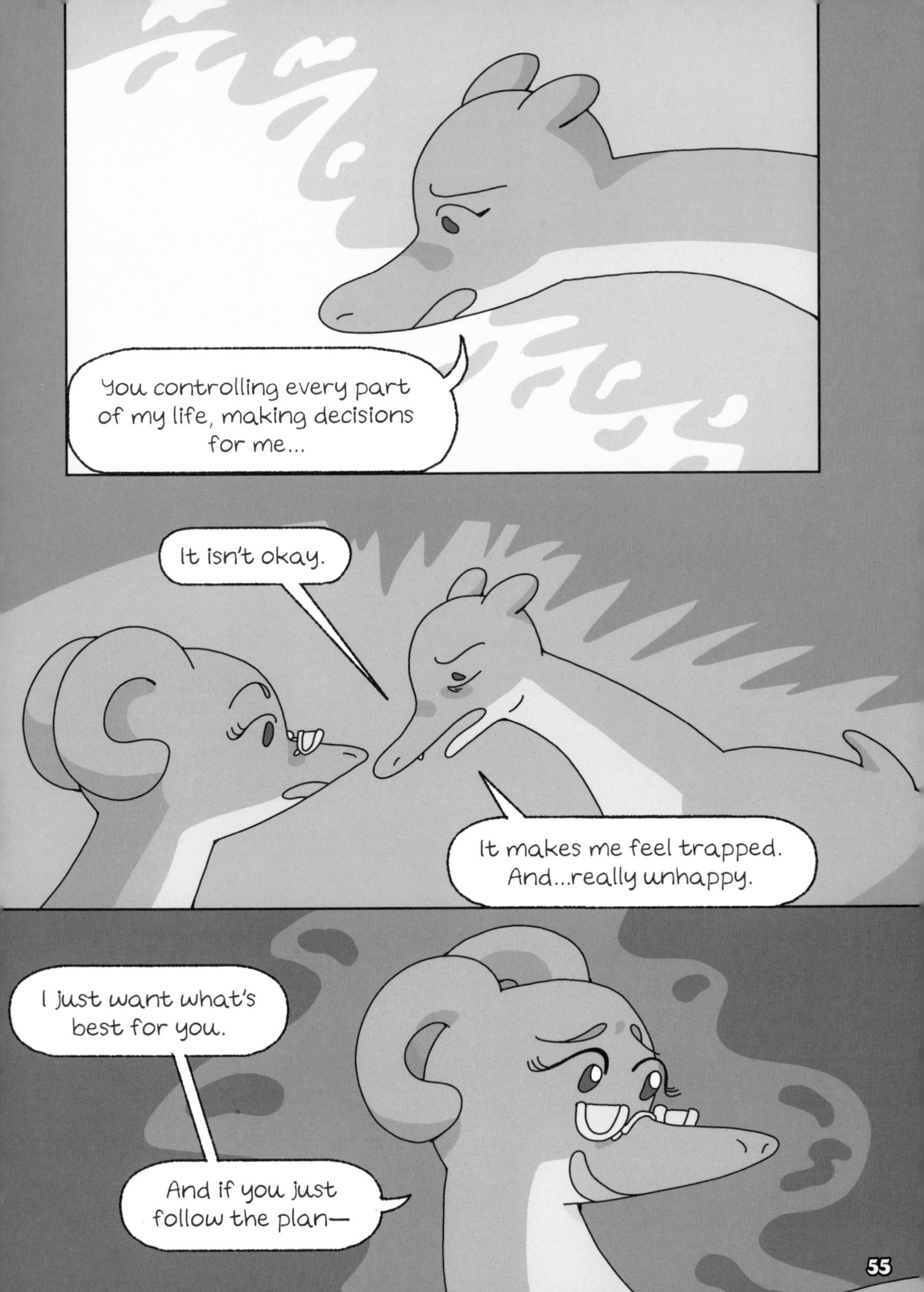
You controlling every part of my life, making decisions for me...
It isn't okay.
It makes me feel trapped. And...really unhappy.
I just want what's best for you.
And if you just follow the plan—

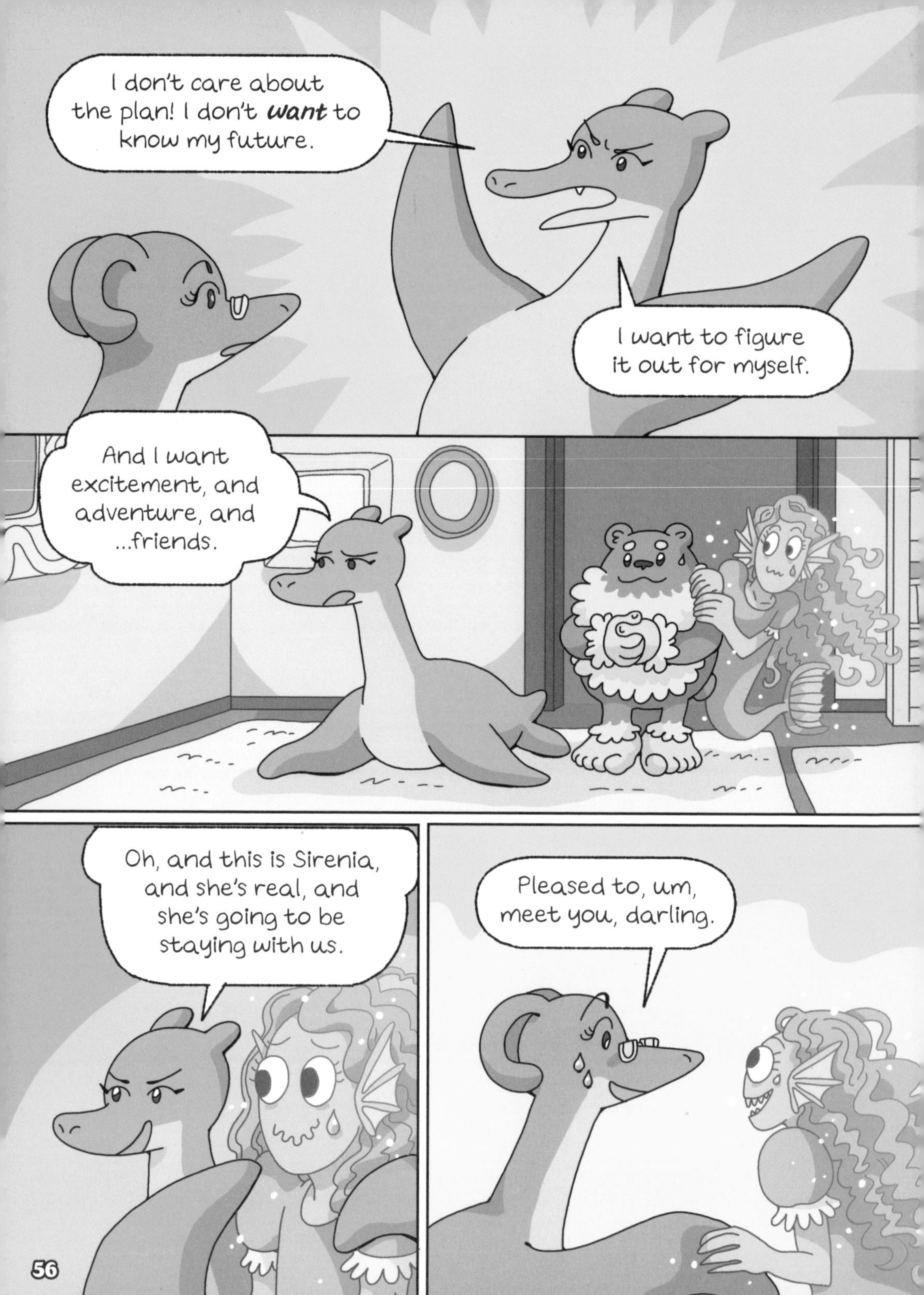
I don't care about the plan! I don't *want* to know my future.
I want to figure it out for myself.
And I want excitement, and adventure, and ...friends.
Oh, and this is Sirenia, and she's real, and she's going to be staying with us.
Pleased to, um, meet you, darling.

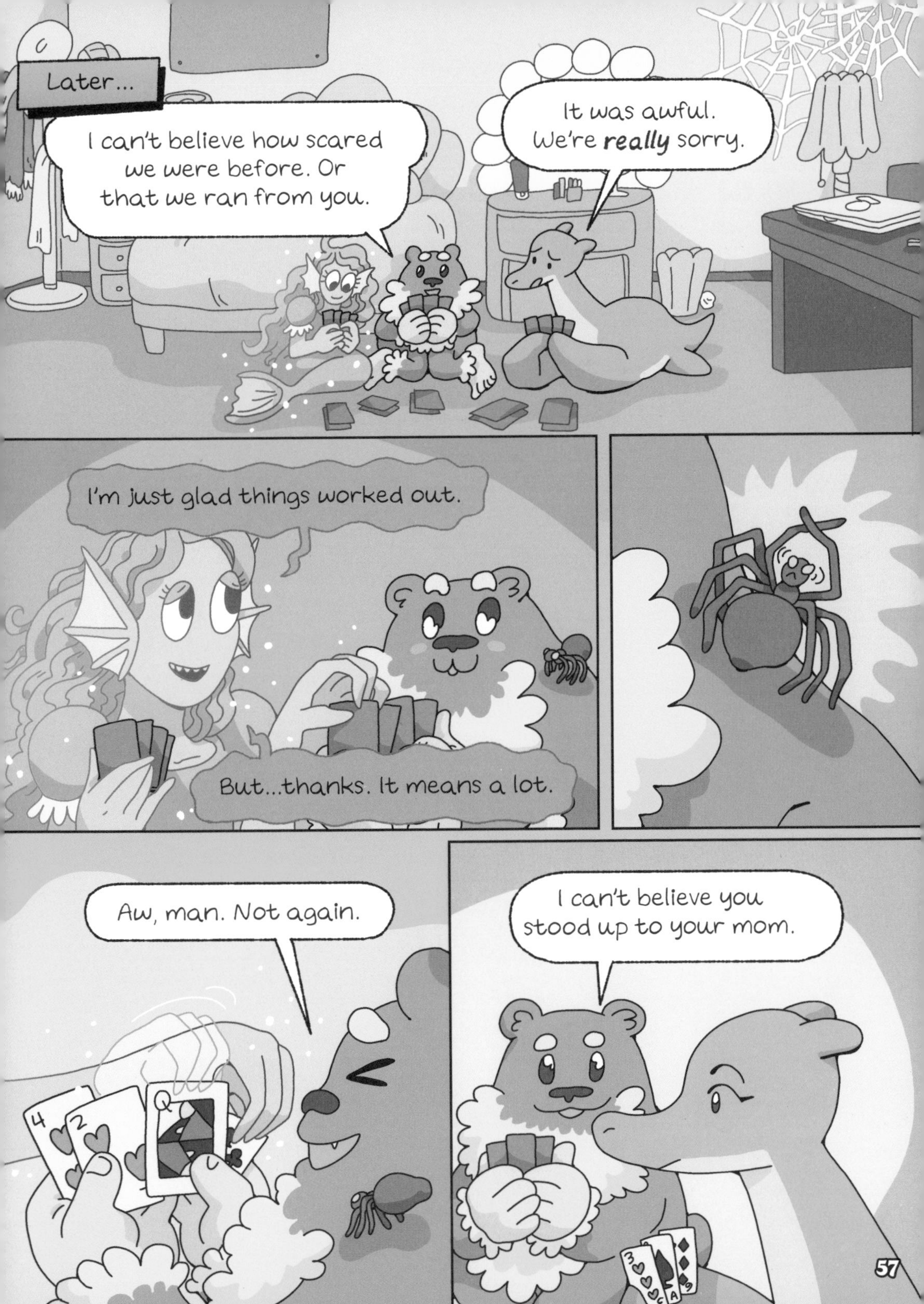

Later...
I can't believe how scared we were before. Or that we ran from you.
It was awful. We're **really** sorry.
I'm just glad things worked out.
But...thanks. It means a lot.
Aw, man. Not again.
I can't believe you stood up to your mom.

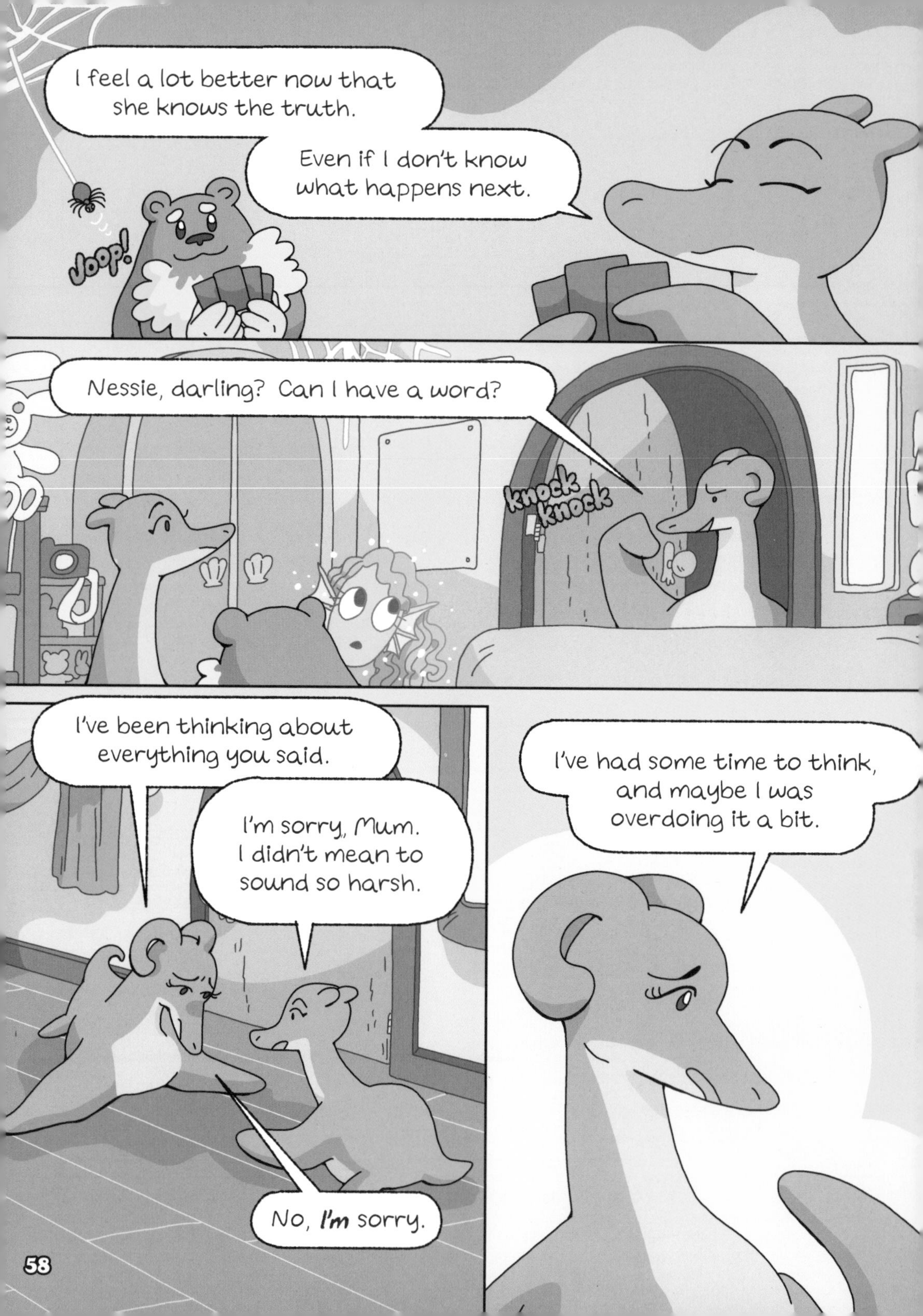
I feel a lot better now that she knows the truth.
Even if I don't know what happens next.
JOOP!
Nessie, darling? Can I have a word?
knock knock
I've been thinking about everything you said.
I'm sorry, Mum. I didn't mean to sound so harsh.
No, *I'm* sorry.
I've had some time to think, and maybe I was overdoing it a bit.

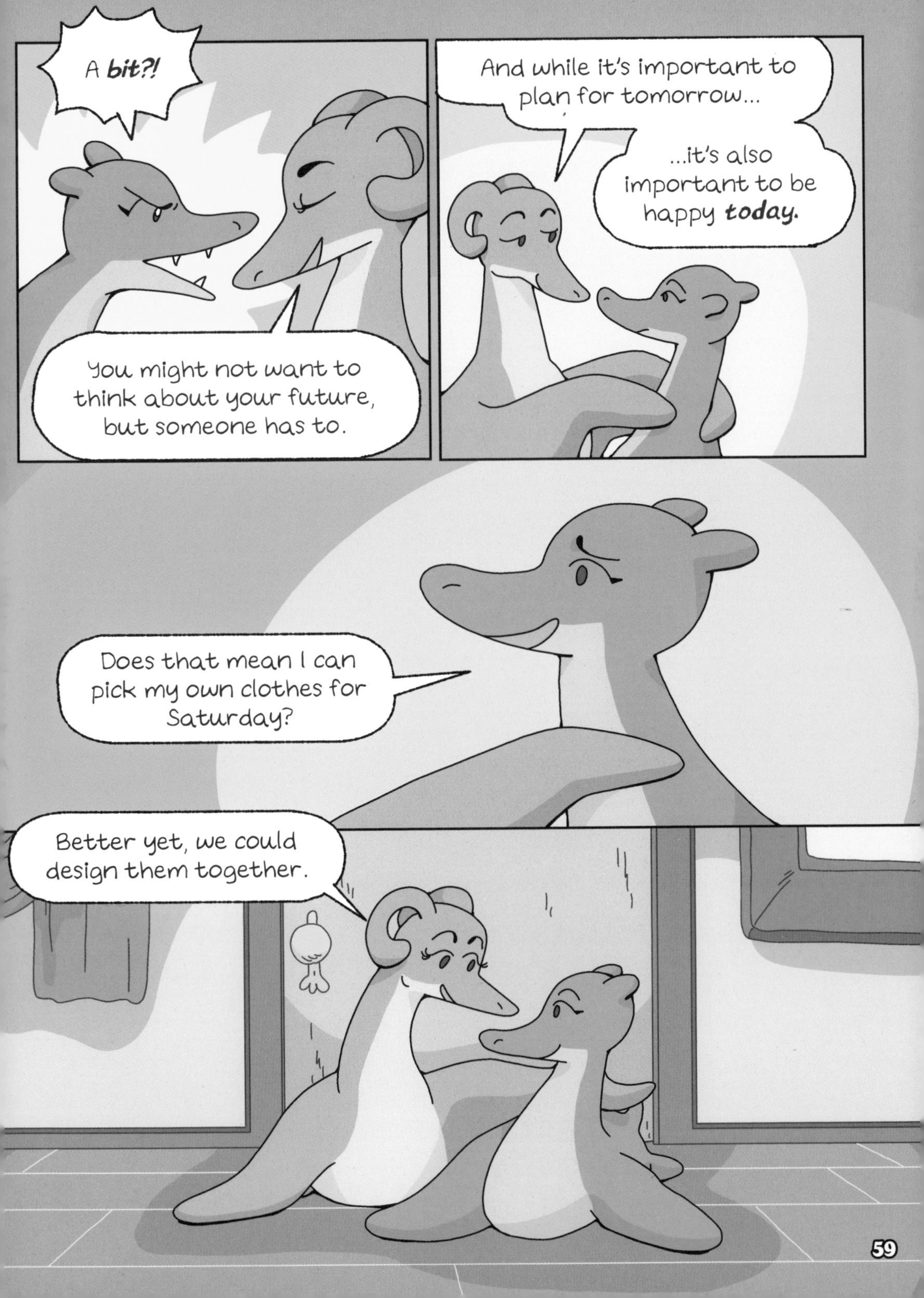
A bit?!
You might not want to think about your future, but someone has to.
And while it's important to plan for tomorrow...
...it's also important to be happy today.
Does that mean I can pick my own clothes for Saturday?
Better yet, we could design them together.

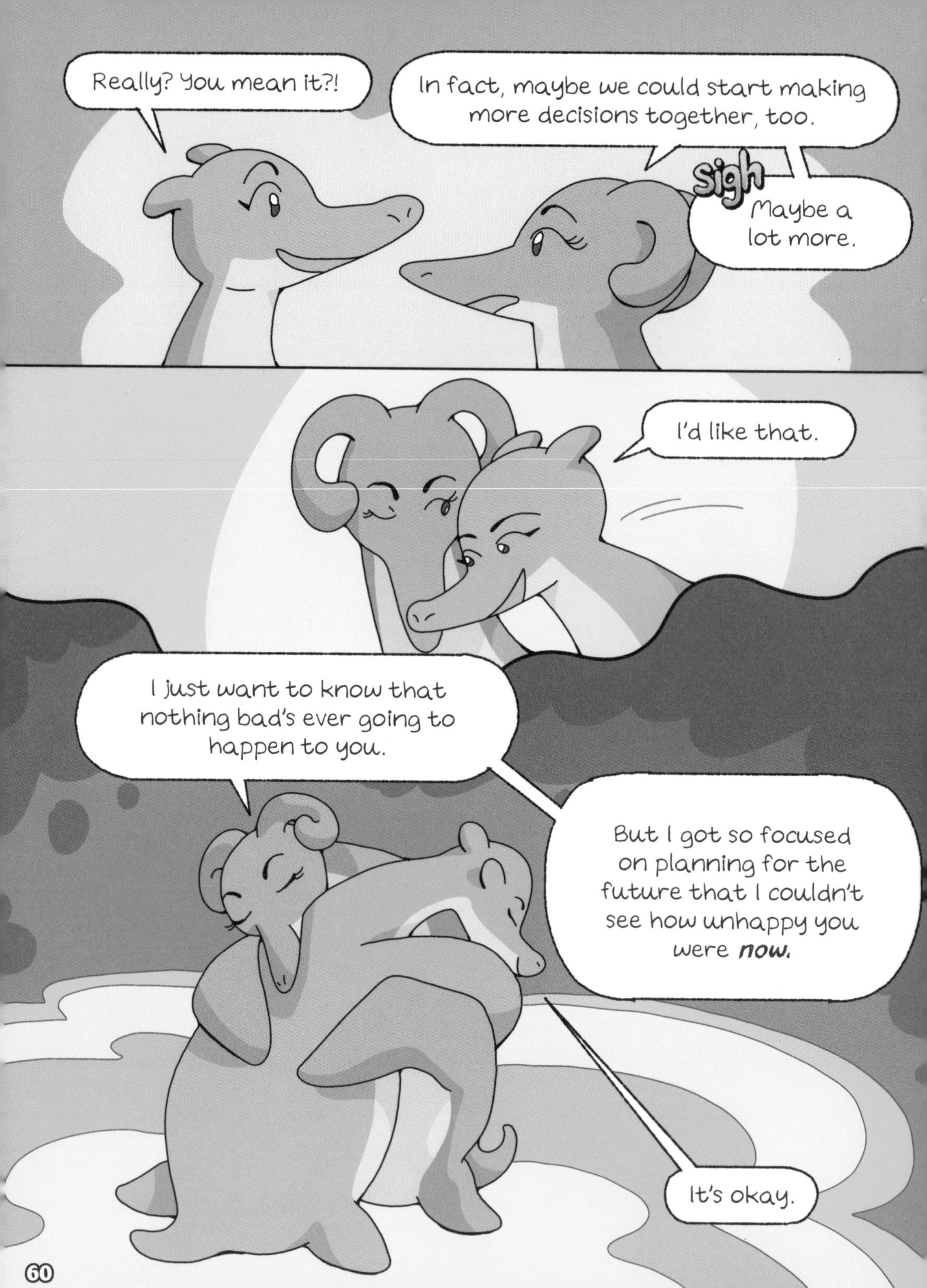
Really? You mean it?!
In fact, maybe we could start making more decisions together, too.
sigh
Maybe a lot more.
I'd like that.
I just want to know that nothing bad's ever going to happen to you.
But I got so focused on planning for the future that I couldn't see how unhappy you were ***now.***
It's okay.

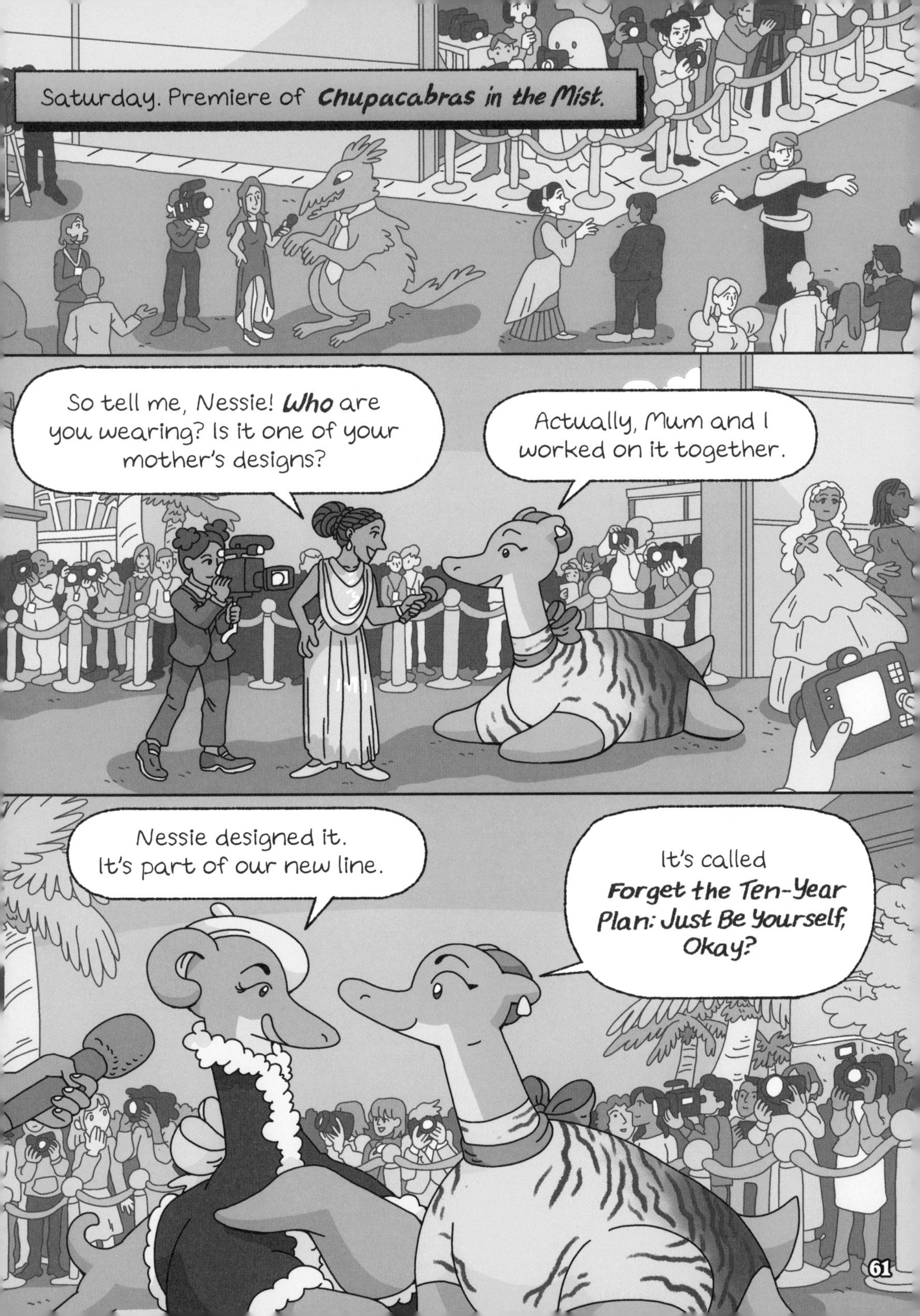
Saturday. Premiere of **Chupacabras in the Mist.**
So tell me, Nessie! **Who** are you wearing? Is it one of your mother's designs?
Actually, Mum and I worked on it together.
Nessie designed it. It's part of our new line.
It's called **Forget the Ten-Year Plan: Just Be Yourself, Okay?**

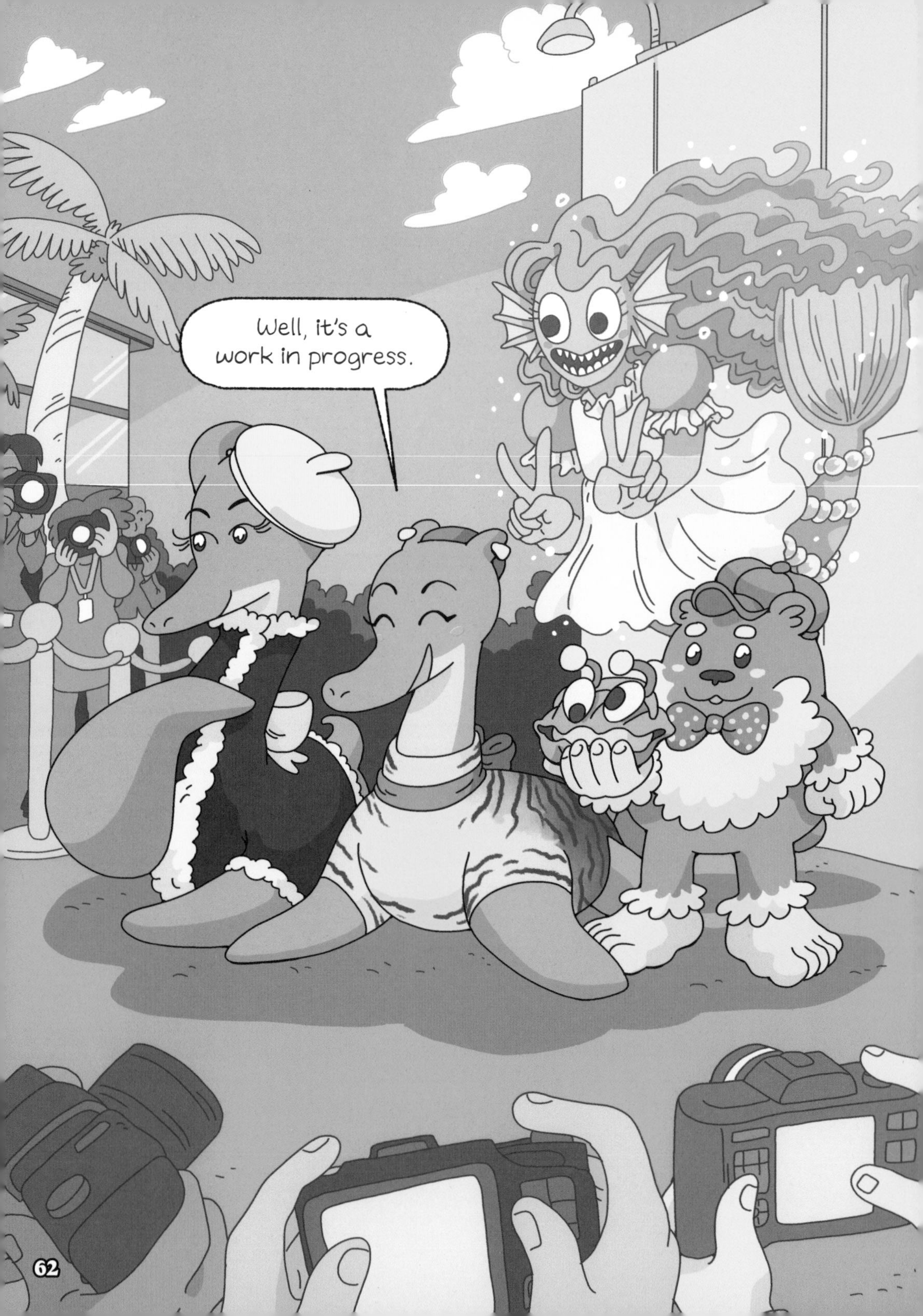
Well, it's a work in progress.

Chloe Tisdale

Chelsea M. Campbell

is always trying new things, which is why she wears a lot of hats. It's definitely not to disguise herself because she's secretly a cryptid. Besides writing this book, she's also the author of the Renegade X series for teens and creator of *The Weaver of Stories* video game. For more information—and to try and see what she looks like without a hat—you can visit her online at www.chelseamcampbell.com.

Priya Alahan

Laura Knetzger went to

the School of Visual Arts and graduated in 2012. Laura started drawing and self-publishing a series of all-ages comics called *Bug Boys* in 2011. Laura loves to make comics and books about small pleasures, small creatures, and feelings. The main inspirations for her stories come from plants and animals, art and handicrafts, and trying to think of things from a nonhuman perspective. She also enjoys painting, playing video games, and knitting. You can find her online at @LauraKnetzger.